Reader

John Simpson

Murder Most Gay

A fantastic story filled with intrigue, humor, sex, action and suspense. Did I mention sex?

—Literary Nymphs

This reader hung in suspense until the very end of the story and enjoyed the read very much.

—Fallen Angel Reviews

Condor One

A brilliant story of "what if" and one I highly recommend.

—Literary Nymphs

Irish Winter

A story so rich in historical detail that reading it is akin to living the actual history.

—Rainbow Reviews

BOOKS BY
JOHN SIMPSON

Condor One
Def Con One
Irish Winter
Murder Most Gay
Talons of the Condor
Task Force

EBOOKS BY
JOHN SIMPSON

The Barracks Affair
Carpathian Intrigue
Four Grooms and a Queen
The Ghosts of Stanton Hall
Naval Maneuvers
Pirate Booty

JACK and
DAVE
John Simpson

Dreamspinner Press

Published by
Dreamspinner Press
4760 Preston Road
Suite 244-149
Frisco, TX 75034
http://www.dreamspinnerpress.com/

Jack and Dave

Cover Art by Dan Skinner/Cerberus Inc. cerberusinc@hotmail.com
Cover Design by Mara McKennen

ISBN: 978-1-61581-419-0

Printed in the United States of America
First Edition
February, 2010

eBook edition available
eBook ISBN: 978-1-61581-420-6

To Jack, the love of my life.

Chapter 1

IT WAS a warm spring day when Dave Henderson was discharged from the United States Marine Corps back into his home community. The sense of freedom Dave felt as he walked down the streets of Reading, Pennsylvania, made him feel light and giddy. He smiled, thinking he would now be able to pursue a career as well as the love life he had set aside because of the military's "don't ask, don't tell" policy.

He had given the end of his teen years to his country, and now it was time that he began planning the rest of his life. He began to relax as he walked down the street and took closer notice of the handsome young guys that passed him, no longer having to be quite as careful with his appraising looks as he had prior to his honorable discharge. Reading seemed to be teeming with really cute guys around his age, and he couldn't wait to hit the many gay bars of the city.

Over the course of the next few days, Dave secured a position as a paralegal in one of the city's premier law firms. While in the Marines, he had begun college and had chosen the legal field as his major. Having completed two years of college in the Marines and currently enrolled in a nearby college, he was desirable by the standards of the local law firms. His current status as a veteran only added additional appeal for other firms. The law firm of Blankenship, Morgan, and Surreal secured his services as a junior paralegal upon the condition that he continued in college and graduated with a degree.

It was Friday night, and he had just received his first paycheck from his new job. It was time to go out and hit the bars and see what Reading had to offer in the way of male companionship. As he

1

wiped the steam off of the mirror, he looked down at his body in the reflection and was very pleased with what he saw. One undeniable benefit of having served in the Marine Corps was the peak physical shape he was required to maintain. His pecs stood out and provided the start for an abdomen that would be the envy of everyone at the local gym. His six pack of abs was almost an eight pack, undeniably a clear selling point for his desirability to other gay men.

His manhood was slightly above average with two rather large balls hanging down like ripe plums in the sun. He refused to follow the trend of shaving his pubic hair and opted instead for a slight trim. He completed his personal inspection by turning around and looking back at his ass. Two cheeks of manly power and beauty were exposed to his gaze, and his legs continued the overall well-muscled look of his body.

Finally, he looked above his pecs and smiled. His light brown, almost blond hair was slightly longer than it had been in the past, shading his bright blue eyes. Strong cheekbones complimented the square jaw that framed his white smile. Now all he needed was the right clothes to show it all off and he had exactly the jeans that would do it.

He walked to the bedroom and went to the closet. He reached unerringly to the exact place on the upper shelf, pulled down a pair of faded 501s and threw them on the bed. From there he went to the dresser, opened his top left drawer, and pulled out his favorite black T-shirt. Next, he took out a pair of black Calvin Klein boxer briefs and some socks.

He dressed—feeling the satisfying caress of his favorite jeans—put on his Marine Corps ring, ran the brush through what hair he had, and headed out the door. He emerged onto the porch of an old mansion house on the main street in Reading. It had been broken up into four apartments, and Dave occupied one of two on the second floor. Beautiful inlaid marble covered the floors, and there was highly polished mahogany wood everywhere one looked.

Dave headed down the street and turned right at the corner headed toward one of Reading's oldest gay bars. The Purple Door had been around for at least thirty years and stood as the symbol of the gay community in the city, and as Dave approached, he had an odd tension in his stomach. Somehow he felt that once he crossed the threshold of the bar, he was identified to the community at large as a homosexual. Considering this was something he had fought against so hard in the military, crossing through the door was like breaking a curse.

When he walked in, all the heads in the place turned to check out who was coming in. The club had a bar formed in a big oval in the middle of the room with a small dance floor off to one side. There was no band, just pre-recorded music played on loop. The light was low, and it took Dave a minute for his vision to adjust to the atmosphere. As he took a seat at the bar, all eyes were still focused on him as the bartender headed his way.

"What'll be?" the cute bartender asked. *Weren't all gay bartenders cute?*

"Rum and Coke, please."

"Sure thing. New around here? I don't remember seeing you before."

"New? Not really. New in here, yes. I just got out of the Marines, and this is my first month home."

"Ah, that would explain the high and tight," the bartender said, referring to Dave's hair.

"Yeah, I kinda like it, though," Dave replied.

"Don't get me wrong, I like it too. Dan's my name," the bartender said, holding out his hand.

"Hi, Dave, glad to meet you."

"Ah, forgive me for asking, but you are twenty-one or older, right?"

"Yep, wanna see ID?"

"Nah, I'll take your word for it. First drink is on the house, Marine," Dan said.

"Thanks, nice of you," Dave replied with a smile that seemed to light up the bar.

As Dave looked around, he found most of the men in the bar were still staring at him. He nodded a few times, and the guys nodded back or waved. It was obvious that more than one man was intensely interested in Dave, but none approached him directly. As he finished his drink, Dan brought another and set it down.

"This is from Nick over there at the end of the bar," Dan said and smiled again. "I don't think you'll be paying for any drinks in here tonight," he continued with a laugh. Dave nodded to Nick and smiled. Dan reached down below the bar and did something that turned up the music slightly. As a good song came on, one young man girded his loins and came up to Dave.

"Care to dance?"

"Hi, I'm Dave," he said, holding out his hand.

"Hi, Dave, Scott."

"Yeah, Scott, I'd love to dance," he said as he slid off the bar stool, took Scott by the hand and headed out on the floor. Only one other couple was dancing so it was easy for everyone in the bar to watch. And Dave gave them something to watch.

It was one of Michael Jackson's hits that almost vibrated Dave off the barstool, and he threw himself into the music. He managed to move in sync with the song, showing off his body in the process. Scott was so captivated by Dave's style that he was just going through the motions, shuffling his feet as he gazed at Dave dancing. As "Wanna Be Startin' Somethin'," continued, a small group of men gathered at the edge of the dance floor to watch. They couldn't take their eyes off of Dave's ass as it wiggled in time to the music. As

Dave got into a dance song, his eyes closed and he became one with the music, unaware that he had drawn an admiring crowd.

A fine sheen of sweat broke out on Dave's forehead as he twisted and turned to the beat. When the song ended, Dave opened his eyes to smile at Scott and found the crowd staring at him. All at once they began to clap, and Scott faded into the crowd.

It must have been Michael Jackson night, because the very next song was "(It Don't Matter If You're) Black or White," and one of the men who had been watching came out to dance in front of Dave. Dave responded by dancing with the newcomer to the delight of the crowd.

As the song wore on, the other man moved in close to Dave and began to run his hands down Dave's back. When the stranger grabbed Dave's ass cheeks, Dave pulled away and left the dance floor. It was obvious that Dave had no intention of being pawed over by anyone.

He found Scott and put his arm around his shoulder.

"You disappeared; what happened?" Dave asked.

"When I found the entire bar watching us, well, watching you really, I became uncomfortable. You weren't alone long," Scott said with a slight frown.

"Ah, pay them no mind. They looked like the seals at SeaWorld at feeding time."

Scott laughed out loud, picturing the seals clapping for more fish to be tossed to them.

"Well, I'm used to walking my dance partner off the floor just like I walked him onto it."

"I'll remember that next time. You know you're hot, right?"

"Not any hotter than a zillion other men."

"Yeah, well, those zillion other guys? They aren't in this bar tonight."

"You say that to all the guys, come on."

"Damn, look at the drinks waiting for you over there! I count seven," observed Scott.

"I guess I ought to drink some of them. Look, maybe we can catch another dance later?"

"Sure, be my pleasure," Scott said.

Dave walked around to the other side of the bar and took his place in front of the stack of drinks. As he looked at them, he motioned for Dan to come over.

"No more drinks please. This enough to get me drunk," said Dave.

"You're not driving, are you?" Dan asked.

"Nah, I only live a couple blocks from here. But please, just tell the guy that I'm not accepting any more drinks, okay?"

"Sure thing, stud," Dan replied with a wink.

Dan removed the one empty glass as Dave pulled a full one toward him. For the next hour, guy after guy came up to Dave and asked him to dance. He accepted a couple of offers but declined most. As closing hour began to near, Dave was feeling the effects of the multiple drinks. The bar was mostly empty now, and Dan began to clear glasses off and announced "last call."

Dave got up and went to the men's room to relieve himself and upon his return to the bar he noticed that it was now two o'clock.

"I guess I can't drink them all anyways. Two left and time is gone."

"Look, I'll shoo the rest of the guys out, lock the door, and you can finish them while I clean up—okay?"

"Sure. I'll hurry."

Dave drank one more but couldn't finish the last drink that had been bought for him. When he got up to leave, Dan came over to him and put his arm around him.

"Did you have a good time tonight?"

"Yeah, sure did. Most of the guys were pretty cool, and I got to dance a lot without worrying if someone from the base was watching."

"Listen, I usually don't do this, but would you like to come home with me and have some coffee?"

Dave looked at the bartender's face and then let his eyes drop down the front of the man. Dave liked what he saw.

"Is that a pick-up line?"

Dan smiled. "Yeah, I guess it is. I would love for you to spend the night with me. We'll wake up, and I'll make you breakfast and drive you home. Whadda ya say?"

Dave stood up and leaned into Dan, giving him a quick kiss which Dan tried to stretch out. Dave was a little drunk and began to sway back.

"Whoa, cowboy, we better get on home before you're on the floor!" Dan smiled as he walked over to the light panel and began to shut off all the lights. After one last look around the bar, he motioned toward the door, and the two men left, Dan locking up behind them.

"How far do you live from here?" Dave asked.

"Not far, we'll be at my place in less than five minutes."

As Dan drove them to his home, Dave looked the bartender over again. Black hair, slender, small waist, big bulge, and cowboy boots—nice. Dave could feel himself growing in his jeans, and he shifted slightly to take the pressure off his erection.

7

After another couple of minutes, Dan pulled along the curb and parked. They got out and went into one of the many brownstone apartment buildings that sat on the outer edge of the city. They went into a first-floor apartment, and when Dan closed the door behind them, he pulled Dave into his arms, giving him a gentle hug and a kiss on the side of his neck.

"Damn, you're one fine man, Marine," Dan said with a heavy laden voice.

"You're not bad yourself, barkeep," Dave replied as he found Dan's lips and pressed a kiss into them.

"Want something to drink?"

"You're off duty now, Dan. But I'll take a glass of something ice cold for the bedroom, if you don't mind."

"We better switch you to Diet 7UP after all that sugar from the Cokes you've been drinking tonight. Come on, kitchen's this way," he said, motioning with his head to the hallway that ran the length of the apartment.

Dave followed and looked around as he went. There was a beautiful old fireplace in the living room and gorgeous wood throughout the apartment. They entered the kitchen, where Dan poured soda into a glass full of ice and handed it to Dave.

"Bathroom is this way," Dan said as he led Dave further down the hallway.

"Here, would you take my drink for me while I hit the bathroom?"

"Sure, take your time."

Dave entered the bathroom and closed the door. After relieving himself, he walked over to the sink, washed off his hands, looked into the mirror, and found two bloodshot eyes staring back at him. *Ugh, you've had too much to drink tonight more than likely, but at least you're gonna get laid for the first time in months!*

He splashed some cold water on his face, which brought about a renewed sense of well-being, and dried off on the towel. He left the bathroom and found the master bedroom where Dan was already lying on the bed naked.

"Damn, cowboy, you don't waste any time, do you?" Dave asked with a smile.

"Well, we both know why we're here and what we want, so there's no sense in being coy," Dan replied while dropping his eyes to Dave's crotch. "Take your clothes off, or do you want the lights off?" he asked.

"No, the lights on are fine for now."

Dave kicked off his sneakers and pulled off his socks without even sitting. Next the T-shirt was peeled off over his head revealing his chest and abs to Dan's admiring eyes. Dan got off the bed, came over to Dave, and said, "Here, let me do that."

Dan got down on his knees and unbuckled Dave's belt, and then slowly popped open each button on Dave's jeans. When he pulled the jeans down, Dave's CKs went with them and out popped Dave's semi-erect cock, bouncing up and down in front of Dan's face. As Dave leaned on Dan's shoulders for balance, Dan pulled each leg of the jeans off along with the underwear.

Dan rocked back on his heels so that he could get a long view look of Dave from head to toe. Dave stood there letting Dan enjoy the view, growing harder under the intense assessment.

"Dave, *you* are incredible. You have one damn fine body, dude!"

"Thanks, that's really nice of you to say."

Dan reached out to touch Dave's cock and balls, gently stroking him. When Dave's cock pointed toward the ceiling, Dan knew that Dave was fully aroused. He rocked forward taking Dave into his mouth, slowly going down all the way to the pubes and releasing him just as slowly as he held his balls.

Dan looked up at Dave and said, "Let's get on the bed."

Dan pulled the covers back to the foot of the bed, exposing the freshly laundered sheets. As they settled down onto the mattress, Dan asked, "Light on or off?"

"Do you have a candle, by chance?"

"Sure do."

Dan hopped out of bed, retrieved a candle, and brought it back and lit it. When the light was turned off, a gentle soft glow made shadows dance on the walls and ceiling.

"You like?" Dan asked.

"Yeah, I like," replied Dave.

Dave took Dan into his arms and began to kiss him while playing with one of Dan's nipples, which immediately became hard. Dan moved one hand down onto Dave's cock and gently jacked Dave slowly as Dave continued to apply kisses all over Dan's neck and chest.

Dan pushed Dave back down on the bed, flipped around and climbed on top of Dave so that they could perform a sixty-nine. Dan eagerly gobbled up Dave's cock once more. As Dave looked up, he saw the beautiful curve of Dan's ass, his balls swinging slightly and his erection pointing out. Dave slid down a little bit, grasped Dan's cock, and pulled it into his mouth as they sucked each other's cocks. Dave rubbed and caressed Dan's ass as he sucked his dick. He let go of Dan's cock and began to run his tongue over the dangling balls before his eyes, jolting Dan upright.

Dan swung over and dropped down alongside of Dave and exhaled heavily.

"Did I hurt you?" Dave asked.

"Hurt me? Hell, no, when your tongue hit my balls, I almost shot my load right then and there. Damn, you know how to use your mouth."

Dave turned on his side, took Dan's face in his hands, and kissed him gently on the lips. "Do you know it's been months since I've been laid? I can't wait to pop one off, so get busy. The head of my dick needs attention."

"Yes, sir," Dan replied.

He crawled down the bed between Dave's legs, and when settled, began to use only his tongue. He ran it up the underside of the shaft and around the head. He licked his way back down and continued onto the heavy sac. He took each ball into his mouth and gently rolled it around with his tongue, making Dave grab the sheets and twist them into clumps. Dan released Dave's balls and went even farther down to the strip between Dave's balls and his asshole. There he licked at a fevered pitch before he grabbed Dave's legs and pushed them back toward Dave's head, exposing the prize he was seeking. Chills ran up and down Dave's body in response to this intimate sexual contact.

Dan licked all around the edge of Dave's opening, which was something no one had ever done to Dave before. When Dan finally hit the middle of the rosebud, Dave saw stars and flashes of light and came up off the bed in pure pleasure.

"Holy fuck! That feels incredible! *Fuck!* Don't stop, please!" he pleaded.

Dan smiled and went back to work on his target. After giving the area a thorough licking, he began to drive the tip of his tongue into Dave's ass. Once again, Dave came off of the bed, taking the sheets with him.

Dan cooled him off a little by leaving the area and working his way back up to Dave's balls. Then he took Dave's cock and went down on him, licking the pre-cum off the tip. He began to go up and down on Dave while playing with both nipples, making Dave moan deeply in appreciation of what Dan was doing to him.

Dan stopped and moved up to look into Dave's face. "Can I fuck you?" he asked. "You've got an incredible ass."

"Ah, I'm afraid not. I'm a virgin that way, and I'm not ready to give that up," Dave answered, knowing that wasn't the truth. Dan had allowed only one other guy to do that, and he would've given his life for that man.

A look of disappointment came over Dan's face. He pleaded some more but was met with the same response. Dave tried to quickly make Dan feel better by pushing him down on his back and begging to suck his cock. The effect of so much alcohol was beginning to take its toll on Dave, and he wanted to finish their sexual liaison before he passed out.

Dave got between Dan's legs, pushed both hands under Dan's ass and lifted him up enough so that he could set Dan's ass on his legs. This brought Dan's cock much closer to Dave's mouth, and he went to work on Dan aiming to bring him to climax.

Dave wet his index finger and worked it into Dan's ass as he sucked Dan's cock with the intent of making him cum. He wiggled his finger in Dan's ass, making Dan moan and move restlessly against the linen. When Dan's balls began to move up to the base of his cock, Dave knew the time was near.

At the first taste of semen, Dave pulled off Dan's cock and began to fist Dan's rigid shaft fast and hard. The climax was now unstoppable, and Dave smiled as stream after stream shot out of Dan's cock, covering Dan's face and chest with white fluid.

When the spurts slowed and finally halted, Dave lowered Dan's ass and slid alongside of the other man, who was breathing heavy and hard. Dave lowered his mouth and kissed Dan's right nipple, causing Dan's body to jerk in reaction. Signaling that his nipples were now oversensitive, Dan covered the right one with his hand and smiled.

Dan reached under the bed and pulled out a cloth that appeared to be used for the very purpose of clean-up. When his breathing returned to normal, he looked at Dave and said, "Now, it's your turn, stud."

Before Dan could move, Dave got up onto Dan's chest and inched forward until his cock was resting on Dan's lips. "Open up, big boy."

Dave eased his cock into Dan's mouth and began to rock back and forth, slowly fucking Dan's face. Dan ran his hands over Dave's ass and parted his cheeks until he could finger Dave's hole. This made Dave increase the speed of his fucking until he felt the climax building. When he was right on the edge, he pulled out and sat back so that Dan could grab his cock and finish him off by hand.

When Dave shot his load, Dan's kept his eyes tightly closed so that the acidic semen covering his face didn't get into them. When Dave finished emptying his balls, he collapsed back onto the bed, chest heaving.

Dan reached for the cloth and wiped his face off. When Dave regained control of his breath, he pulled himself back to lie alongside of Dan and smiled.

"Damn, that was fine. You have no idea how bad I needed to bust a nut, dude."

"Oh, I felt how bad, believe me." Dan laughed.

Dan got out of bed and went into the bathroom. When he returned to bed, Dave smiled at him sleepily, practically snoring. Dan smiled and said, "Well done, Marine, well done."

He pulled the covers up and blew out the candle. Within a minute, he was fast asleep too.

Chapter 2

THE next morning, after getting dropped off by Dan, Dave climbed the steps to his apartment and headed into the bathroom to get the laundry basket. It was Saturday, and that meant it was laundry day.

After putting the first load into the washer, Dave put on the coffeepot, sat down at the kitchen table, and thought about the night that had just passed. The sex was good; Dan was good-looking and the hangover slight. All in all, a pretty damn good night out on the town. It was Saturday; did he want to go out again later that night? His thoughts were interrupted by a knock on his door. Since it wasn't the doorbell from the main front door, it had to be someone from one of the other apartments.

When Dave opened the door he found a twenty-something guy standing there with a bottle of wine in his hand.

"Hi," Dave said.

"Hello. I saw that you just moved into the building, and I thought I would bring by a little housewarming present for you to welcome you to your new home," he said with a smile.

"Ah, so you live in the building?"

"Just down the hall. We have the two apartments on this floor."

"I was just doing laundry, but you're more than welcome to come in and sit down for a few minutes."

As the pleasant-looking guy came in, he said, "I'm Ron, by the way," he said while sticking his hand out.

"I'm Dave, pleased to meet you. Please sit down," said Dave as he indicated the sofa with a wave of his hand. "Would you like some coffee since it's a little early to pop open that bottle?"

"That would be great. Black, please."

"I'll be right back with the coffee," Dave said as he got up and went to the kitchen. He poured a cup of coffee for Ron, grabbed his own, filled it, and headed back. "Here you go," he said as he sat down once again.

"Thank you. With that hair, I'm guessing you just got out of the Army or something, right?" Ron asked with a smile.

"Marine Corps actually."

"A Marine? Whoa, that'll liven up the neighborhood."

"Excuse me?" Dave asked with a puzzled look on his face.

"Oh, I just mean that with all the gay men that live in the area, you're gonna draw a lot of attention. I suppose you dislike gay men?"

"Actually, no. I take it that once you learned I was a Marine, you automatically assumed that I'm an intolerant asshole who beats up gays for fun on a Saturday night?" Dave asked, his face flushing slightly.

"Oh, I didn't mean any offense! I just mean, well... yes, I guess you're right. I'm sorry for jumping to conclusions, but we hear so many stories in the community."

"We? So, you would be one of these gay people who live around here?" Dave asked.

"Well, you might say that. In fact, you might say that the entire building you're living in is gay. All gay men. The apartment buildings on either side of us are also full of gay men. That's why I said you're gonna attract a lot of attention looking the way you do."

"And what way do I look?"

15

"Well, you gotta know that you're a very hot-looking dude. You've got the body, the face, the muscles; my God, you're practically every gay man's wet dream!"

Dave laughed out loud. "I've been called many things in this life, but a wet dream has not been one of them. If I *was* an asshole, that kind of statement might get your ass beat," he said with a smile.

"So, you're not pissed at me?"

"No, I'm not pissed at you. In fact, I'm gay also."

"Holy shit! You're kidding; your gorgeous ass is gay? Are you single?" Ron asked as his eyes dropped to Dave's crotch.

"I believe that more than just my ass is gay," Dave replied. "Yo, my eyes are up here, dude," he continued to get Ron's eyes off of his junk.

"Oh, I'm sorry again. It's just that you're so hot; I mean everyone's been talking about you since you moved in. You might say that I'm the advance recon party. There, did I say it in terms you would understand?"

"Another assumption is that Marines are dumb. Wrong. I understood you perfectly."

"I seem to be saying I'm sorry all the time to you. Again, I don't mean anything offensive. You didn't answer my question, though."

"Question?"

"Are you single?"

"Yes."

"Oh my God."

Dave broke out laughing. "Are you this way with all the guys that move into this building?"

"No, just former Marines who look like you," Ron cooed.

"Well, I put my pants on like every other guy, one leg at a time."

"Could I see that?"

"Could you see what?"

"You putting on your pants."

Dave laughed again. "You need to go and take a cold shower and let me get back to my laundry."

"If I must, okay," Ron said with a smile. "Look, the guys would like to throw you a little welcome party, if that would be okay with you?"

"Yeah, sure, I'm cool with that."

"How about next Friday night, say, in my apartment?"

"Next Friday night it is. Thank you very much," Dave said with a smile that would soon become famous.

Ron shook hands with Dave and left the apartment. Dave stood where he was for a moment, laughed again, and took the wine into the kitchen. This was going to be an interesting place to live.

The week flew by, with Dave spending more and more time in court assisting one of his attorneys as a paralegal. He enjoyed being in the middle of the action and wanted to specialize in the criminal work that was one of the firm's specialties. However, before he was able to specialize, he was required to learn the overall practice of law as performed by his firm. True to his nature, he didn't complain but applied himself to learning and looked forward to the day when he would be arguing cases on his own.

On Friday afternoon, he finished a criminal brief and left the office just after five p.m. and walked the seven blocks to his apartment. One advantage to living in the city was that he could walk to almost any place you needed to be.

He got his mail from the mailbox and jogged up the stairs to his apartment. As he put the key in the lock, Ron popped his head out of his door.

"Hi, Dave. Is eight o'clock tonight all right for you?"

"Yeah, sure is. I'm gonna take a bath now and relax a little; work was busy today. I'll come over at eight."

"Great, can't wait."

"Can I bring anything?"

"Just yourself," Ron said with a wave of his hand, and he was gone.

Dave smiled at his neighbor, entered his apartment, threw the mail down on the coffee table, and headed into his bedroom to change. After stripping off his clothes and hanging up his pants, he collapsed naked onto the bed. Then he got up, flicked the ceiling fan on, and fell back onto the bed. As the gentle current of air moved across his body, Dave closed his eyes for just a second.

An hour later, a loud siren going past the building woke Dave up. He sat up with a jolt and looked at the clock. It was now 7:05, and he was still in need of a bath or shower. He jumped off the bed and went to the bathroom, forgoing the comforts of a hot bath for the utilitarian benefits of a shower. He scrubbed every inch of his body in anticipation of meeting someone hot at the party and having company through the night.

He dried off, turned off the coffeepot, and went back to the bedroom. What to wear? He pulled out a pair of black jeans and a white polo shirt that would accentuate all of his best features. He decided to go commando, skipping underwear to give that added enticement to any who might be inclined to look for other assets that Dave possessed.

He put on a thin gold chain and a ruby ring given to him by his grandfather. He chose black socks and black loafers to complete his wardrobe for the evening. The final touch was two hits from the bottle of Polo cologne on his dresser. It was now 7:36, and he was ready to party.

Dave went into the bar area and poured himself a small scotch on the rocks to sip until it was time to venture forth into the land of lions and tigers. As he sat in his living room, he could hear the voices of various men walking up the stairs and down the hallway to stop at Ron's door. A knock gained them entrance almost at once. He heard the happy voices of friends gathering together for an evening of drinks and conversation.

Realizing that he would not really know anyone at the gathering with the exception of Ron, whom he hardly knew, Dave felt a little butterfly flitting around in his stomach. As the clock on the fireplace mantle rang eight o'clock, Dave stood up and checked himself out in the mirror one more time. The fireplace had a beautiful mirror cut into the wall over the mantel, making a last minute check easy.

Happy with the way he looked, Dave made sure he had his key and left the apartment to walk down the hallway. Before he could knock, the door opened, and Ron was there to greet him.

"Right on time, just like I knew you would be," Dave's neighbor said with a smile.

As Ron stepped aside, Dave entered the apartment through a little hallway that led to the other rooms. "This way, everyone is waiting to meet you," Ron said with a giggle.

As they entered the room, all eyes turned toward the newcomer. Their expressions were friendly and welcoming.

"Everyone, this is the guest of honor, Dave from 2A, our newest resident here at 1039 Penn Street."

Dave was inundated with hands seeking his, slaps on the back, and multiple voices talking at once. As Dave was talking to one of the men, Ron shoved a rum and Coke into his hand with a wink. Dave wondered how Ron knew that this was his particular drink.

After Dave sat down in a chair, he counted fourteen men in the apartment. One of the guys helped Ron serve various finger foods, and it was only then that Dave realized he hadn't eaten dinner and was, in fact, starving. When a plate came around with meatballs and shrimp on it, Dave took a few pieces of each and placed them on a small plate he had been given.

Everyone wanted to hear stories about what it was like to be a Marine and if he had been able to sleep with everyone under the rank of major while on active duty. To their disappointment, Dave painted a picture of hard work, dedication to duty, and very little time to search for intimate male companionship.

Steven, one of the guys Dave was first introduced to spoke up and said, "You made quite the impression at the Purple Door last weekend. I hear you met Dan?"

"Were you there?"

"No, I'm afraid I was out of town, damn it."

"Well, how in the hell did you hear about that?"

"Oh, you know, guys will talk, and you were the hit of the bar, I understand."

"Yeah, well, I had fun."

The conversation was thankfully interrupted by a latecomer. Ron brought him over to meet Dave.

"Dave, this is Jack Stonner. He's one of the guys who live in the next building."

"Ah, pleased to meet you, Jack. Glad you could make it," Dave said.

"Thanks, glad I could come; sorry for being late. Had a little problem with my roommate in getting out for the evening."

Dave made a mental note of that. What kind of problem would this really cute guy have leaving for a couple of hours? "Is he your lover?"

"No, just a roommate. It's a long story," Jack said with a slight frown.

"Excuse us, Dave, while I take Jack to get a drink. We'll be right back," Ron said.

Dave watched as the blond man, who was wearing jeans so tight they looked like they were painted on, walked down the hall. He had beautiful blond hair, blue eyes, about a thirty-inch waist, and a very fine-looking ass. He also was obviously packing a dangerous weapon in his pants, from what Dave could briefly tell. Jack looked to be about twenty-five-years-old and had a very sweet look to him. Dave's antenna went up to full mast. He liked what he saw.

There were more than a few good-looking men at the party, but the one thing they were missing was any kind of real personality. When Jack and Ron returned, Dave squeezed over to one side of the chair and motioned for Jack to sit down next to him. As skinny as he was, both men fit in the chair, although it was a bit tight.

When everyone else got lost in conversations with others, Dave decided to find out more about Jack.

"So, what's the deal with your roommate? Why did you have trouble getting away tonight?"

"Oh, he thinks I'm his boyfriend and that he can tell me what I can do. He even tries to tell me what I can read. He doesn't like it if I read a sex book or something like that."

"But he's not your boyfriend?"

"Nope."

"Why does he think that you are?"

Jack leaned over to Dave and whispered into his ear. "I let him blow me, and he thinks that makes us boyfriends and gives him rights."

"Ah. Do you do him back?"

"No."

"Does he knock on your back door?"

"Huh?"

"Does he fuck you?"

"No, I'm a virgin there."

"I see. What was his objection to your coming out tonight?" Dave asked with interest.

"He's afraid I'll meet someone I like."

"Oh, I see. He might lose control over you?"

"Yeah, 'fraid so."

"Do you wanna get a drink sometime?"

"Sure, although you look like you're pretty popular," replied Jack.

"Not to sound conceited or anything, but I'm kinda used to it now. I go out with who I want. By the way, you look great in those jeans."

"Look who's talking! I can tell what religion you are just by looking down."

Dave cracked up laughing drawing the attention of everyone in the room. "Touché, Jack, you got me there."

"So where do you work?" Jack asked.

"I'm a paralegal in a local law firm. You?"

"I work at the DMB bank, down on Penn Street. I'm an assistant accounts manager there."

"You like it?"

"It's okay, I guess."

"Time for pictures everyone," announced Ron. "Come on, Dave; come over here and pose with the guys," he urged.

Dave got up and walked over to the standing group and got in the middle of them all as Ron took various shots of the men. When he put the camera down, everyone broke back up into small groups, and some of the guys got ready to leave.

"Ron, one more picture if you don't mind. Jack, come over here, please," said Dave.

When Jack stood next to Dave, Dave put his arm around Jack, and Ron took the picture.

"Make sure I get a copy of that will ya, Ron?" Dave asked, and he saw Jack smile.

The party began to break up a little after eleven p.m. as some of the guys were heading out to the bars and others were heading home with someone else from the party. Dave walked Jack out of the building and over to his. At the entry, Dave stopped Jack before he put the key in the door.

"Come here, you."

"What?" Jack asked with a smile as he got close to Dave.

Dave put his arms around Jack, hugged him and then gave him a quick kiss on the lips. "Thanks for talking with me tonight. I enjoyed your company. I'd like to see you sometime; would that be possible?"

"Sure. Give me a call?"

"You bet. What's your number?"

Jack reached into his wallet and pulled out a business card. "Call me at the office. That way I don't have to worry about anyone listening in on our conversation."

"Great. I'll call you this coming week."

"Good night, Dave," Jack said with a smile as he opened the door and went into the apartment building.

Dave walked back to his building, thinking of how pleasant it has been talking with Jack. He liked him and wanted to do more than see him again. He would have to thank Ron for putting on the party after all. Instead of being bored and anxious to leave, he might have found a new friend and for that, Dave was grateful.

Dave looked at his watch and decided to hit a different bar tonight. He didn't need anything from his apartment so he walked the block and a half to a different gay bar than the Purple Door. Tonight, he would check out the Lone Star, a semi-Western-type bar.

When he walked in, he found a large room with the bar in the middle in the shape of a horseshoe. There were several pin ball machines around the bar, and the bathrooms were at the very back. Sawdust covered parts of the floor, and there was a very tiny dance area just to the right of the entrance.

Dave took a seat at the bar, ordered a rum and Coke, and casually glanced around the room. There was a mixture of young guys and older men talking to each other and playing the machines. In contrast to Dave's first visit to a Reading gay bar, hardly anyone here paid much attention to him. One or two men took notice of the newcomer, but they went right back to their drinks after a once-over.

When the bartender, who had a name tag on that read Sam, served Dave's drink, he asked the same question Dan the bartender at the Purple Door had asked. "New around here?"

Dave smiled and just said, "Yes."

"Welcome then. Hope to see a lot more of you in the near future."

Sam walked away to sling some more beers down at the other end of the bar and left Dave alone to enjoy his drink. The music was low so that you could talk to someone if you wanted to without straining your voice. The sound was definitely country and Western.

"Buy you a drink?" asked a man who was at least thirty years older than Dave.

"Got one, thanks anyway," Dave replied with a smile.

The guy walked away, apparently used to that type of response. It was then that Dave saw a handsome young guy in the corner with a build similar to his own. The stranger had black hair and light-colored eyes. Dave couldn't tell exactly what color from this distance in the low lighting.

The guy caught Dave checking him out and nodded. Dave smiled and turned back to his drink, trying not to be too obvious that he was interested in the man. Over the course of the next hour, Dave and the guy played cat and mouse, which eventually got old for Dave. Just after one a.m., Dave took his drink and walked over to the pinball machine next to the cutey that he'd been flirting with for the past hour.

After setting his drink down on a ledge next to the machine, he put in a quarter and began to play. As he began to play, the man with the black hair finally made his move.

"Hi, you new around here? I haven't seen you before, and I know I would remember if I had," he said.

"Yep, moved into the city a little over a month ago now. I'm Dave," he said as he held out his hand.

"Pleased to meet you, Dave; I'm Derrick. You look really fine in those jeans you're wearing, by the way."

"Thanks, you're looking rather hot yourself. It's hard to tell in here with this light and smoke, but what color eyes do you have?"

"Hazel. Yeah, it is really smoky in here—gets to me after a while," Derrick said. "I especially hate it when I get home and my hair and clothes stink from the smell. I usually take a shower right away. Can I buy you a drink?"

"Thanks, Derrick, but I think I've had enough tonight. I'm nursing this one, and I might have a glass of Coke and that's it."

"You wanna come home with me tonight?" Derrick asked with a smile.

"You wanna get fucked tonight?" Dave asked boldly.

"Fuck yes, dude! Let's get out of here now. We'll take my car, and I'll bring you back when we're done."

"We might not be done all night. What then?" Dave asked with a smile.

"Then I'll be taking you out to breakfast, dude."

"Let's go," Dave said.

After they got into the car and began to head toward Derrick's house, Derrick turned to Dave and asked, "So are you a cop or military?"

"I just got out of the Marine Corps, and I now live in Reading. In fact, I live just over a block away from the bar."

"A Marine, huh? Hot."

After a ten-minute drive, they pulled into a slightly upper-scale apartment complex on the outskirts of the city. They walked up one flight of stairs and entered a very modern-type apartment. The furniture was fairly new, and the house was immaculate.

"Real nice place you got here," Dave commented.

"Thanks, I try. You wanna drink? You're not driving, after all."

"Sure, same as the bar. Rum and Coke, if you have it."

"I have it. I have other stuff, too, if you want a change."

"Nah, I've got one of the stomachs that if I mix liquors, I end up getting sick. So, I stick to one kind of drink and that's it."

"No problem, I'll make us drinks and be right back. Sit down; make yourself comfortable. In fact, kick off your shoes, if you like."

"Thanks, I will."

While Derrick was in the kitchen, Dave looked around on the walls and saw family photographs showing he had brothers and what appeared to be a lot of friends. Then he came to a picture he wasn't expecting: Derrick was a cop. There in a silver frame was a picture of Derrick graduating from the police training academy, looking incredibly hot in his police uniform. When Dave heard Derrick coming, he sat back down on the sofa.

"Here ya go. Let me know if it's too strong."

Dave took a sip and found it perfect. Derrick sat down next to him on the sofa and said, "You are one hot motherfucker. You know that, right?"

"Have you looked in the mirror? You looked good in the bar, but you are one fine man in the light too!" Dave said, and they both laughed.

"So what do you do now that you're a civilian?" Derrick asked.

"I'm a paralegal with a downtown law firm. It's also my major in college—law that is. I'll have a B.A. in law when I'm finished."

"Will you go to law school?"

"I'm not sure. I don't have any plans for that, but you never know in life what's going to happen."

"Like meeting you tonight. I was looking at the same old tired faces that come into the Lone Star week after week, and then I saw you sitting there. Frankly, you took my breath away."

Dave leaned over and kissed Derrick for the compliment. "That's nice of you to say that. I must admit that I wasn't impressed with the crowd either until I laid eyes on you."

"That was really hot; the way you asked me, *do you wanna get fucked tonight*? I was like, damn! This man knows what he wants!"

"And you said yes. Can we do something about that?" Dave asked.

"Sure," Derrick said as he leaned in for a longer kiss. "But first, can we have a little fun by taking a shower together? We both reek of smoke, and I'd really rather not smell that when we're in bed together."

"Agreed. Lead the way."

Derrick took Dave by the hand, and they made their way to the bathroom where they stripped off their clothes, each man checking the other out. Neither was disappointed in the unveiled body of his bedmate for the evening.

They got in the shower and washed each other's backs and even shampooed their hair. When they got out of the shower, Derrick took a towel off the rack and dried Dave off completely before Dave returned the favor.

"Just leave your clothes in here for now. Let's get our drinks and go to the bedroom," Derrick said.

As Derrick walked by Dave to lead the way, Dave gently slapped him on the ass and said, "That is one fine piece of ass you got there, stud."

Derrick laughed and said, "Well, let's see if you like it even better in an hour."

They got their drinks and headed into the master bedroom, where more photographs of Derrick corroborated the fact that he was a police officer. They talked about it briefly, finished their drinks in bed, and then turned the lights out. For the next hour and a half, Dave and Derrick thoroughly enjoyed each other's bodies during the time they spent together. Dave found that Derrick was even better built then he was, and Derrick explained that he worked out four days a week.

"That was fantastic, Dave. Nice to be made love to by a man who knows what he's doing."

"It was easy with a man as fine as you."

"Wanna sleep here, and we'll go out for breakfast, and then I'll take you home?"

"I'd like nothing better."

They fell asleep in each other's arms, and both slept better than they had in some time.

Chapter 3

DAVE got back to his apartment a little after ten the next morning and found a note slipped under his door by Ron.

> *Hi, Dave, hope you had a great time last night. All the guys loved you and are in love with you! A couple of the guys wanna go out with you, so if you're interested, let me know and we'll talk. Hope to see you around soon!*
>
> *Love, Ron*

Dave folded the note and put it into his desk drawer to remind him to write a thank you note for the party. He'd had a good time, but it got a lot better when Jack came into the picture. Damn, he'd looked good in those jeans of his!

WEDNESDAY arrived, which for Dave meant four hours at college and away from the office. He had two classes on Wednesdays, one that ended at eleven in the morning and another that started at one in the afternoon. This meant he was alone for two hours on campus during lunch time.

As his morning class ended, Dave headed to the phone and pulled out the business card Jack had given him. He dialed the number, hoping that Jack was in his office.

After three rings, Jack answered. "Hello, this is Jack."

"Hey, Jack. Dave here, from the party the other night. Is this a good time to chat for a minute?"

"Sure, glad you called. Are you at the office?"

"No, today is my class day. I'm out at Dupree with two hours to kill until my next class."

"Really? Well, it's almost lunch time here. Why don't I drive out there to meet you, and we can eat lunch together?"

"That would be great; I'd love to see you again. When can you leave?"

"I could be there in say twenty minutes. Is that good?" Jack asked.

"Sure, that'd be great. I brought a sandwich from home, and we can get sodas in the cafeteria here and then take a walk along the treeline that borders the campus."

"Sounds great. Look for me pulling into the parking lot, okay?"

"You bet. See you shortly!"

Dave smiled broadly when he hung up. Just the thought of seeing Jack again made him happy for some reason. He walked to his locker and got his lunch and headed to the parking lot to wait for Jack. He passed a lot of cute boys on the way but didn't pay as much attention to them as he normally would. He was remembering meeting Jack at the party and how good it felt sitting so close to Jack in the chair.

About ten minutes later, he saw a blond-haired man behind the wheel of a car and knew that Jack had arrived. Dave ran up to the car and opened the door.

"Hey, you really made good time getting here!" Dave said with a smile.

"Yeah, traffic was good today. Nice to see you again," said Jack.

"Same here. Come on; let's grab a soda and eat. How long can you stay?"

"I've got about fifty minutes, and then I gotta get back to the office."

"Good, wanna eat while we walk?"

"Sure, where can we get the soda?"

"This way," Dave said as they walked toward the admin building near the football field. They got their sodas and walked to the trees where they could talk without being overheard.

"I enjoyed our talk Saturday night," Dave said.

Jack chuckled. "We didn't really get that much time to talk. The other guys were hanging around you like bees on honey. But, yeah, I enjoyed meeting you even though I got a bunch of shit when I got home."

"From your roommate?"

"Yeah, he was being a real dick. Demanding to know who was at the party and who I talked to. He wanted a full report."

"What did you tell the asshole?"

"Told him I was tired and I went to bed."

"Why do you put up with it? If he isn't your boyfriend, he has no right to question you like that."

"I need the roommate. Rent is a little high for me to handle alone, and so I put up with it."

"You want me to talk to him about this shit? I'll straighten his ass right out," Dave offered.

"No, that will only cause trouble. I just ignore him and he eventually gives up."

"You said you let him blow you?"

"Yeah, well, I get horny, and it's also kind of a benefit I give him for paying the utilities and to shut him up. He wants to be lovers, but I'm not interested in that."

"How often do you give it to him?"

"Every couple weeks, so it's not too bad. I'd rather not, but that's how it is."

"Well, enough of him. How come a cute guy like you doesn't have a *real* boyfriend?" Dave asked.

"I might ask you the same thing. Everybody's tongue hangs out when you're near, and I've heard you're not shy about sampling the goods, but you haven't bought anyone yet."

It was Dave's turn to smile. "I need the whole package, not just a body. Most of these guys have the personality of a wounded moose. You spend what? An hour, if you're lucky, screwing in bed, and the other twenty-three hours you have to sleep, eat, and talk with the guy. Besides, I need a guy that is emotionally compatible with me."

"What does that mean?" Jack asked.

"I'm kind of an alpha male, and I need someone that isn't. If I took up with another alpha male, I'd kill him or vice versa. My future boyfriend and partner in life needs to be mellow and easy to get along with, because I know that I can be difficult at times."

Jack looked at his watch. "Well, I'd better get going. I've enjoyed eating with you," Jack said as he smiled at Dave.

"Can we maybe make this a weekly thing?"

"Sure, I'd like that," Jack responded.

Dave waved as Jack drove away. As he headed to his next class, he felt particularly happy for some reason. He knew he liked Jack, but was he just going to be another sexual conquest like all the others had been up until now? Jack had said that he had "heard" that Dave wasn't shy about sampling the goods; was Dave getting a reputation for sleeping around? It was true that Dave hadn't been alone many nights since getting the apartment. Well, what was a guy supposed to do?

WHEN Saturday night rolled around again, Dave decided not to repeat his usual behavior by going out to hunt for the next trick. Instead, he went over to Jack's building and rang his apartment doorbell.

The door buzzed, and Dave entered looking for apartment 4, the number on Jack's mailbox. He climbed the stairs to the third floor and found someone standing in the open doorway to the apartment.

The guy looked about 26 years old, had short, black hair, brown eyes, and was marginally attractive. "Yeah, what are you looking for?" he asked in a far-from-friendly manner.

"I'm looking for Jack; is he in?" Dave asked.

"Who are you?" the guy asked.

"Is he here or not?"

"He might be; now who are you?"

"I'm Dave, and you are?"

"I'm Billy," he said as he looked Dave up and down.

"You gonna answer my question? Is Jack here?"

"I'll see," he said, closing the door and leaving Dave standing in the hallway at the beginning of a slow burn.

After a few seconds, Dave heard raised voices coming from inside the apartment. The noise didn't quite rise to the level of a fight, but it was clear Billy wasn't happy that Jack had a visitor. As Dave was getting ready to pound on the door, it opened and Jack appeared.

"Hi, everything okay?" Dave asked as he tried to look past Jack to see where Billy was.

Jack rolled his eyes and said, "Yeah, everything is fine. He's just upset that you came to see me."

"This is asinine. You're an adult; you can damn well see who the fuck you want to see in your own home."

"Shh, don't make things worse."

"Look, I came over to ask you if you wanted to catch the midnight show at the movies. Whaddaya say? You up for it on a Saturday night? My treat."

Jack looked down at the floor and after a second looked back up and smiled. "Yeah, that sounds like a lot of fun. Lemme get my wallet."

"Can I come in and wait rather than stand out here in the hallway like the hired help?"

Jack smiled again, opened the door, and walked back to what Dave assumed was the bedroom. Dave closed the door and stayed on his feet, listening for the slightest hint that something was going to get physical.

"Where are you going this late?" Dave heard Billy ask Jack.

"I'm going out to the movies; I'll be back later," Jack replied.

"What? No, you're not. You tell him that it's too late and that you're going to bed. Tell him now!"

"Ouch! Get your hand off; you're hurting my wrist!" Jack exclaimed.

That was all Dave needed to hear. He pushed the bedroom door open and found Billy holding Jack by the wrist and twisting it.

It was a bad move on Billy's part. Billy's eyes grew wide when he saw Dave standing within a foot of him. Jack opened his mouth to say something, but he didn't get the chance to utter any words.

Dave swung a right hook that landed just under Billy's jaw, lifting him up off the floor slightly and tumbling him backward onto his ass. Dave stood over the prone man with a look of murder in his eyes and said, "Keep your fucking hands off of him. Do you understand?"

"Dave, it's all right, really. I'm not hurt. Just let him be, please," Jack implored Dave.

Dave didn't take his eyes off Billy, silently daring him to get up and do something. Billy was smart enough to remain on the floor and not move.

"If I ever hear you put your hands on Jack again without him asking you to, I will finish what I just started. Do you understand me, boy?"

No response came from Billy.

"Do you understand?" Dave asked while taking a step closer to Billy.

"Yeah, I understand. You had no right to hit me," he replied.

Dave looked down with contempt and turned to go with Jack. When they got outside, Jack made it known how he felt.

"Dave, I didn't need you to do that. I don't need a knight in shining armor to come along and save me. You know that right?"

"I never said that you did, but that asshole has no right to hurt you or try to hurt you, especially on my account. Who the fuck does he think he is anyway?"

"I told you. He thinks he's my boyfriend."

Dave turned his head and spit onto the grass in response. "I hate bullies and that ass clown is a bully. If he wants to get physical with someone, he can do it with me, and I'll clean house with his ass."

"Look, you're getting more upset. Please calm down or I'm going back to the apartment."

"Okay, okay. Can we forget it for now and try and enjoy ourselves tonight?"

Jack exhaled the tension he was feeling deep within him and smiled. "Yes. But after this, you're buying the popcorn!"

Dave laughed loud enough that a couple on the other side of the street looked over. They walked the four city blocks to the local theater and went in even though they were almost an hour early. As promised, Dave bought Jack popcorn, and also a soda, two boxes of chocolates, and some nuts. For himself, Dave bought a soda.

THREE hours later, standing outside of Jack's apartment building, Dave asked, "Do you want me to come in to make sure you're going to be all right?"

"No, I can handle things. You get to bed. It's late."

"Call me if there is any problem. You promise?" Dave asked.

"I promise. Good night," Jack said as he stole a quick kiss from Dave and entered his apartment building. Dave turned around and walked next door to his own building with a good deal of worry about this guy that was having a strange effect on him.

After an hour in which the phone didn't ring, and the doorbell was quiet, Dave decided he could go to bed. As he climbed into the bed and drew the sheet over him, he wondered what it would be like to have Jack in bed with him. But what was funny to Dave was that he wasn't just thinking of fucking Jack and going onto the next conquest. This one, he might want him to stick around for a while.

TEN o'clock the next morning, Dave couldn't resist any longer. He picked up the phone and dialed Jack's number, fully prepared to insist on talking to Jack, but he was surprised when Jack answered the phone.

"Jack, you okay?"

"I knew it was you. Yes, I'm fine, as I told you I would be. Billy isn't even here this morning. He went over to his family's place for Sunday church and dinner later."

"Sunday church the day after he tried to hurt you. He needs churching, but I'm surprised the roof doesn't fall in on him!"

"You know, for such a butch guy, you sure can be a drama queen!"

"Please tell me that you did not just call me a drama queen!"

"Wait a minute." Jack paused, trying to control a grin. "Yeah, I checked, and I did just call you a drama queen."

"You wait 'til next time I have you alone—I'll teach you to be respectful to your betters!"

Jack laughed and said, "Promise?"

It was Dave's turn to laugh now. "Promise. Okay, well I had to check on you to make sure things were cool."

"Everything is good. By the way, he's got a purple lump on his chin."

"Serves him right. He's lucky I didn't break his damn jaw!"

"There you go again! I'll talk to you soon, cupcake!"

Before Dave could respond to the cupcake remark, Jack had hung up. Dave smiled. He really liked this guy. Dave began to think of a plan to get Jack out of the city and away from all this so that they could have some quiet private time together and maybe make love. After thinking about it for a while, he realized the perfect spot would be Atlantic City, where the action never stopped!

Over the next couple of weeks, Jack met Dave for lunch on Wednesdays at the college, and they talked about everything under the sun. Dave enjoyed himself just being with Jack *and* without anyone's clothes coming off! This truly was a first for Dave.

He wasn't living the life of a monk, however, and on the weekends when he wasn't talking to Jack, he was out in the bars looking for his next conquest. A new club had just opened in the city, and the grand opening night was by invitation only. Dave had received one in the mail, and Saturday night was the big event.

After taking a shower, Dave went to his closet to figure out what he would wear. He decided against the jeans look as this was the opening night for a gay *club* and not merely a bar. He decided on a pair of charcoal grey slacks that hung just right on him, a black belt with a gold buckle, and a white long-sleeved Polo shirt. Black loafers and the usual gold adornments completed the look. He passed on all of his sweaters in the belief that the club would be hot by the end of the night. Dave planned on being there at the end of the night if the club was even close to being a hit.

As he left his building, he looked left to see if Jack was outside, but he wasn't. He continued the seven-block walk until he arrived at Oz, where two bouncers were checking invitations at the door. Dave showed his and entered what was the center of the city, at least for that night.

The club was filling up with all types of men and a few women. As usual, Dave drew admiring looks from all quarters as he walked up to the bar and ordered a rum and Coke. He strolled around the club, checking out the layout as well as the men. He was attracted to several of the guys, and it was obvious that the best of Reading's gay scene had been invited. Dave wondered how he'd managed to make it onto the list.

The club was designed to resemble the old-time nightclubs of the early decades of the twentieth century. Tables and chairs with linen tablecloths surrounded a dance floor that was laid out in front of a stage. Unlike many others, the new club served food so that you could bring a date or friend for dinner, then dance, and end the evening with a show. Dave had to admit he was impressed with the concept.

He found a table one row back from the dance floor and took a seat. It was a little two top along one wall with a candle lamp in the middle of the table.

Half a dozen men were out on the dance floor, and Dave became lost in the movements of one couple who really knew how to dance. He admired their footwork, watching the curves of their asses as they moved in time to the music. It was obvious that this couple had danced many times together as they were in total sync.

Once again, he scanned the room and spotted two men making their way from table to table, chatting with the patrons. He assumed that they were the managers or owners.

"Hello, I'm Franklin Venchenzo. I'm the owner of this club, and I want to thank you for coming tonight," the taller of the two men said with a smile.

"Hello, I'm Dave Henderson. Thanks for the invitation. You got a beautiful club here, and I think it can't help but be a hit with the community. You can arrive at eight or so, have dinner, and stay the entire night. Smart idea."

"Well, that's my hope for the club. Why go anywhere else when you can find it all here in one place? The food will be good, the drinks reasonable, and the music hot. I hope we'll see you here often."

"Thank you, Mr. Venchenzo. It's very likely."

"Are you all alone tonight?"

"Yes, I came alone."

"How's that possible? A good-looking boy like you? You should have men dripping off of you by now, if men are your thing that is...."

"Oh, I imagine I'll make some friends tonight before I leave," Dave said with a broad smile.

"Well, I'd like to think you've already made a friend," Venchenzo said with a smile. He made his intentions quite clear with the look he gave Dave as he turned and continued onto the next table. Dave noticed that the guy looked back a couple of times as he was scanning the crowd.

Fifteen minutes later, a waiter arrived at the table with a bottle of Dom Perignon and a bucket. "With the compliments of Mr. Venchenzo," he said as he popped the cork, poured a glass of the champagne, and placed the bottle into the ice.

Dave sat there stunned for a moment and then looked around to see if the man was watching, but Venchenzo was nowhere to be seen. Dave looked around at the other tables to see if anyone else had wine or champagne at their tables. They didn't.

He sipped the champagne and found the taste much to his liking. Looking at the bottle, Dave knew he would be drunk by the end of the evening if he tried to drink it all alone. The waiter returned with a second glass, set it on the table, and walked away. Now if Dave wanted someone to join him, he could offer them a glass of champagne.

This time when he looked toward the entrance to the show room, he found his benefactor standing there looking at him. Dave nodded in thanks to Venchenzo, who nodded back and smiled.

After everyone had a few drinks, the crowd began to loosen up. Young guys began to come up to Dave's table and flirt. Dave was enjoying himself immensely when Venchenzo returned, effectively shooing one suitor away.

"Are you enjoying the Dom?"

"Very much, thank you. It really wasn't necessary however," Dave replied.

"The only things necessary are death and taxes." Looking at the dance floor and seeing it fairly full, he turned back to Dave and asked, "Would you like to dance? It's a slow one for the moment."

"Yes, I would love to," Dave responded.

As they walked to the dance floor, Dave noticed that the man who had been walking around with the owner was now at the room entrance watching them. When they got to the center of the floor, Dave asked the question that began to concern him slightly.

"Is that your boyfriend watching us?"

"Boyfriend? Who?"

"The guy who was with you when you first came up to me at the table. He's watching us now."

"Oh, no, that's Louie, he works for me. Boyfriend?" Venchenzo laughed loudly and pulled Dave in close to him. "You know you're one of the finest young studs I've seen in a while. I can tell from holding you that you have a smoking body. Am I right?"

"Ah, thanks, yeah, I just got out of the Marine Corps, and so I'm for sure in shape."

"A Marine? I should have known. You look like a Marine. What do you do for a living now that you're out?"

"I'm a paralegal at a local law firm."

"Yeah? Anything else?"

"Yeah, I'm also in college to finish my degree in legal services."

The music ended much to Dave's relief as he was becoming a little uncomfortable. Venchenzo walked Dave back to his table and found that three guys had taken over the table and pushed the champagne aside. Before Dave could say anything, the owner bent over and told the guys they were sitting at a private table and that they needed to leave.

Since they had no idea who Venchenzo was, they responded like fools. "Fuck off. The table was empty and now it isn't. Go find another table," the largest guy said.

"Move now," was the only response from the owner.

The guy who was getting mouthy stood up and took an offensive stand, and before Dave knew it, Louie and two other rather large men were at the table removing the interlopers forcefully but quickly.

"I'm sorry, David. Please sit."

"Maybe I shouldn't keep a table all to myself when you're this busy."

"Nonsense. You can have any table in the house. You are my guest. Now please sit back down and enjoy the champagne. Or would you rather have something else to drink?"

"No, no, this is more than fine. Thank you, sir."

"Please, call me Franklin. You're not in the Marines anymore," he said with a smile.

"Okay, Franklin, thank you."

"Think nothing of it." He turned and walked away as Dave sat there trying to figure out exactly what was going on. He felt like a beautiful woman who was being hit on by the ugly old troll who was rich and used to getting what he wanted. The display of muscle that appeared as if by magic also was of some concern. It was obvious that there was more to what he was seeing than was evident.

By the time he was near the end of the bottle of champagne, and the hour was nearing two a.m., Dave's eyes became heavy. He got up from the table and headed toward the exit of the club when he was intercepted by Louie.

"Mr. Venchenzo would like to see you," the brooding man said.

"Oh? Sure, I wanted to thank him before I left anyway. I'm afraid the champagne has gotten to me a little bit."

Dave followed Louie through a door and up a flight of stairs that led to the second floor of the club. They entered what appeared to be a very private second club, complete with another bar and six tables. The atmosphere was very intimate as well as secluded. When they walked into the main room, they found Franklin Venchenzo sitting at a table with a woman and two men. When he saw Louie and Dave, he told the others to leave the table.

"The gentleman was about to leave," Louie said to Venchenzo.

"Ah, so soon? Would you like to continue to enjoy yourself up here? Here *closing time* has no meaning."

"Actually, Franklin, I must decline. I'm afraid the champagne was not only outstanding, but strong. I need to go home and get to bed. But I appreciate your hospitality tonight, and I wish you a lot of success with the club," Dave said with a slight slur here and there.

"Would you like some coffee first? Maybe help you get your bearings some?"

"No, sir, I really need to go to bed."

"Ah, very well, David. It has been a pleasure to meet you tonight. May I call you sometime?"

"At the moment, I can't even remember my new phone number. I'm sorry."

"Very well. Louie, would you show David the way out and make sure he gets outside unmolested? Also, see to it that David gains entrance to the club any night he wishes... no line for him, understand?"

"Of course, Mr. Venchenzo," Louie said as he took Dave's elbow and guided him back down the stairs to the first floor. As

Dave felt the fresh air hit his face outside, he breathed a sigh of relief. He'd felt for a few moments that he was going to end up in leather restraints and put into a sling! The seven blocks that it took to get to the club now seemed like seven miles. Dave saw a cab and hailed it and rode home. He stumbled up the stairs, fought to get his key in the lock, and fell into bed fully clothed. He didn't wake up until late morning, and when he opened his eyes, pain struck his entire head. Dave had a class-A hangover.

Chapter 4

DAVE managed to crawl out of bed and make his way to the bathroom where he relieved himself, opened the medicine cabinet, took four aspirin, and returned to the bedroom. This time, he managed to get his clothes off *before* climbing under the covers. It was too late when he realized that he had forgotten to close the drapes, and instead of trying to get out of bed to close them, opted to hide his head under a pillow.

Just after three o'clock, Dave woke up and found that he felt a little better, but he was still not up to his usual self. He was able, however, to get out of bed, slip on a pair of boxers, and make some coffee.

After his second cup, he actually began to feel much better. As his mind cleared, he began to think of the one person who held his interest: Jack. He wondered what Jack was doing and if he was okay. Dave decided to call and find out.

To his disappointment, Billy answered the phone.

"Yeah, put Jack on the phone," Dave said.

"Who's calling?"

"None of your damn business, just put Jack on."

"Oh, it's you."

Dave heard the handset drop onto the side table, and Billy screamed out for Jack to get the phone. After a minute, Jack picked up.

"Hello?"

"Hey, it's me, Dave. How are things?"

"Hey, okay. It's funny you called. I was just thinking about you."

"Yeah? How come?"

"Oh, was wondering if you went out to the new club opening last night," Jack replied.

"Ah, yeah, I guess I did. Got pretty wasted on a free bottle of champagne, and my head is killing me today. Hell, I just got up."

"They gave out free champagne?"

"No, just to me I think. It was Dom Perignon and it had the year 2005 on the label. Boy, it was good going down. Wish you had been there to share it with me. Maybe my head wouldn't be ready to explode."

"Who gave you the champagne?"

"The owner of the place. It was weird. He was, like, coming on to me, but not really... if you know what I mean. Anyway, I drank nearly the entire bottle and left, feeling no pain."

"You went home alone? That's front page news!" Jack said with a chuckle.

"Smartass. I don't get laid every time I go out, you know."

"Sure. I also know the guys are lined up waiting to get into your pants, but that's to be expected with your looks."

"Okay, enough about that. You wanna grab some dinner later?" Dave asked.

"Ah, I can't. Billy has been making dinner all day. I think he's trying to impress me, and if I bail on him now, there'll be war."

"Fuck that guy, man. Okay, maybe next weekend?" Dave asked with hope.

"Sure. How about Saturday night at this new club?"

"Ah, lemme think about that. If the guy at the club really does have the hots for me, it might be awkward showing up with you. I'm not sure what to make of this guy, to tell you the truth. I get some vibes that he might be bad news."

"Okay, well, you decide. I'm game. See you Wednesday on campus?"

"I sure hope so. I look forward to our talks."

"Okay, see you then."

Right after hanging up, the door bell rang. Dave jumped up, left his apartment, and ran down the stairs to open the outside door. He found a florist standing there making a Sunday delivery.

"Mr. Henderson?"

"Yeah?"

"These are for you, sir. Please sign here," the guy said, pointing to the paper on his clipboard.

"Who are they from?" Dave asked with a puzzled expression, abruptly realizing that he was standing there in his boxer briefs.

"I'm not sure, sir. I just got called in to make the delivery."

Dave took the large floral bouquet and went back up to his apartment. He set the arrangement on the table and pulled the card out.

David,

Hope you had a great time at the club last night and hope to see you back this week.

Warm personal regards,

Franklin

Dave sat down on the sofa, stunned. He looked back up at the bouquet of at least two dozen roses along with several other types of flowers and then read the card again. Something began to turn in his stomach. Dave became very uncomfortable and didn't know how to react to the flowers. It wasn't even like it was just a small arrangement; it was huge and obviously expensive. This Franklin guy was trying to impress his way into Dave's pants.

He picked up the phone and dialed Jack.

"Hello?" Jack said.

"Jack? Dave. Can you pop over here for a minute? I wanna show you something I just got and get your opinion of it."

"You're not just trying to stir the pot up over here, are you?"

"No, seriously, I need your advice."

"Okay, I'll be right over."

Dave got up and walked around the flowers as if they were a land mine and went back down to let Jack in. He waited for a minute before Jack came bouncing through the door.

"Hey, what's up? You sounded a little worried."

"Lemme show you."

Dave closed the door and made sure it had latched. They went up the stairs and when Dave opened the door to the apartment, Jack saw the flowers and gasped in surprise.

"You're kidding. You got those?"

"Yep, a couple of minutes ago."

"Who sent them?"

"The guy from the club," Dave said, handing Jack the card to read.

After reading the card Jack looked back at the flowers and whistled.

"Well, they *are* beautiful... if overdone," Jack said.

"What should I do?" Dave asked with a worried look.

"Thank him?"

They both sat down on the sofa and stared at the large arrangement that was now creating a wonderful floral aroma in the living room. The arrangement was so large that it blocked Dave's view of the television. The only place in the apartment that it would fit and not be in the way was on the floor in front of the fireplace. After a couple moments, Jack spoke up.

"Look, I'm in charge of business accounts for the bank, and I know that the club has several accounts with us. I have to review the accounts as a matter of routine. I can't tell you anything I find by looking at the accounts because of Federal bank secrecy laws, but what I can do is tell you simply, I'm worried or I'm not worried. If I'm worried, then there is something that is bad for you personally. I'm not sure what that would be, but I won't know until I look. I would also suggest that you put distance between you and this Franklin. Don't go back to the club is my advice."

"Fuck, this could get sticky. What about the flowers? Shouldn't I thank him for them? To not do so would be rude and show disrespect, and I have a feeling that disrespect is the last thing one would want to show this man. You pick up certain instincts in the Marines, and one of them is an instinct for danger. I felt it last night, and I feel it even stronger today."

"Fine, send him a note. Perfectly legitimate, proper, and safe. That way he can't get you involved in a conversation where he invites you to do something and you have to decide whether or not to accept the invitation."

"Yeah, you're right. Great idea. I'll write a note today and mail it in the morning. He asked for my phone number last night, but I told him I was too drunk to remember my new number. He actually had me stopped by this goon as I was leaving, and I had to say goodbye to him before I got out of the club."

"Oh, that's not right. You ever see reruns of an old television series called *Lost in Space*?"

"Hmm, I don't think so, why?"

"There's a line from that show that is very appropriate here: 'Danger, Will Robinson, danger!'"

"Shit, I don't even have anything like a note card or a thank you card. I can't use a sheet of paper. There would only be about a dozen words on it, and it would look stupid."

"Don't worry. I have something at my place. Lemme go get it and I'll be right back."

"Thanks, Jack. I really appreciate your advice on this."

"No problem," Jack said with a sweet smile.

After five minutes Jack returned with the perfect note card that had enough room on it to put down a polite thank you and not much more. Jack helped Dave with what to say, and the card was sealed, and Dave took it to the mailbox immediately.

LATE on Tuesday, Dave got called into the office of the senior law partner, Andrew Blankenship. As Dave went in, he tried to settle his nervous stomach thinking that he was in trouble. Why else would the senior partner—who was also the managing partner—of the firm want to see him?

"Ah, Dave, come in, sit down."

"Thank you, sir."

"I wanted to tell you that there will be a little bonus in your paycheck this week, so don't be surprised when you find your check a little larger than normal."

"A bonus, sir? What did I do to earn a bonus?" Dave asked.

"We picked up a new client today because of you. Franklin Venchenzo, who owns a new club in the city called Oz, asked us to represent him in all of his legal affairs. That could be anything from zoning issues to criminal matters. He said that you recommended the firm to him, and that he was quite taken with you. Bringing in new clients is the job of the partners and not junior staff so a bonus is called for in this case. If we have any papers that need to be signed or transported to him, we'll send you to take care of it. Thank you, Dave. Keep up the good work," he said as he got up to shake Dave's hand.

Dave left the office, shaken, and headed home since it was his normal time to leave anyway. He found himself looking over his shoulder all the way home to see if he was being followed. Dave was certain that he hadn't told Venchenzo where he lived or worked; yet flowers were sent to his apartment and Venchenzo was now in contact with his employer.

This is fucked up!

When he was back in his apartment, he dialed Jack's number. Dave was told that Jack wasn't home from work yet. Billy didn't offer to take a message and just hung up.

Frustrated, Dave sat down to think this all out. Should he call Derrick, the cop he went home with the other night? Should he tell Derrick what was going on and get his advice? Dave got the feeling that talking to the police, even unofficially, wasn't a good idea. He was sure Venchenzo would be super-pissed off at him should he learn of it. Dave was certain he didn't want this man mad at him.

The doorbell rang, and Dave went down to answer the door cautiously. What would he find this time? When he opened the door, he broke out in a smile.

"Hey, sexy, thought I would pop in on my way home. How was your day?"

"You won't believe this. Come on. Let's go upstairs, I don't wanna talk about this in a public area."

"Oh dear," was Jack's only response.

After Dave told Jack all that had happened at the office, Jack sat back and looked worried.

"By chance, I ran across the accounts for Oz today. I'm worried."

"Great. This gets worse and worse. Fuck, maybe I should just go down there and tell him I'm not interested."

"Tell him you have a boyfriend," Jack suggested.

"Can't. I already told him I didn't have one."

"That means this is all an attempt to get you into bed... or more. Actually, I doubt he would be doing all this just for sex. He wants more, I think."

"Like what, my firstborn?"

"Like being his partner, his lover!"

"But he doesn't even know me! How the hell could he want me as a lover after one dance and a few minutes of conversation?"

"You know very well that many men like trophy wives and girlfriends. It's a status thing. Did he make any remarks about your looks?"

"Lemme think. Shit, yeah, he did. He called me a stud, if I remember right."

"That's what this is, Dave. He's hunting for a trophy boyfriend, and I think the kinda circles he travels in are not all that healthy for gay men."

"What should I do?"

"Avoid him at all costs, for starters."

"That might not be possible. My boss told me today that I would be the one to deliver or pick up papers from him that involve his representation by the firm. He's pretty damn smart, when you think of it. If he can't get me socially, he'll see me on my job, and he knows I can't refuse."

"Can you talk to your boss?"

"I'm gonna have to. This is the very last conversation I wanted to have with my employer. My sex life is none of their business, and now I have to make it their business. Hell, I could get fired. In most of the states, there's no protection from being fired just for being gay. Fuck!" Dave stood up and pulled Jack to his feet. He put his arms around Jack and hugged him tightly. When he broke the hug, he kissed him lightly on the lips.

"Wow, what was that for?"

"For being here when I need your advice. Sure, I've had a few dates since I've been back, but you're the only one I look on as a friend that I trust."

"Well, if that's how you kiss a friend, it's no wonder you don't have any friends," Jack said with a smile.

"Oh?" Dave pulled Jack back into his chest and kissed him firmly, slowly working his tongue into Jack's mouth.

When they parted, Jack smiled and said, "Now *that* was a kiss!"

"You should see what else I can do with my mouth."

"Would one of those things be eating? I'm hungry. Let's go out for a quick bite to eat somewhere."

"Can we use your car?"

"Sure, where do you wanna go?"

"Let's go out of the city to that little restaurant in Mt. Penn. We shouldn't run into anyone there that I would rather not see at the moment."

"Sounds like a plan. Let's go."

AFTER dinner, they drove up Mount Penn to The Pagoda, which sits high up on the peak. After driving for several minutes, they arrived at the seven-story brick and tile structure built in the Japanese architectural style. It sat almost nine hundred feet above the city and when lit up could be seen from all over the area.

They got out of the car and strolled to the edge of the walkway and stood along the railings looking out over the city. A nice breeze blew through their hair, and Dave felt some of the tension easing from his body.

"I like it up here," Jack said.

"Yeah, it's very peaceful. Wanna get something to drink from inside?"

"Nah, I'm full from dinner, but you can if you like."

"No, I'm good too. I wish I could hold your hand up here. But I know we can't."

"Not yet and we'll probably never live to see it either," Jack sighed.

After ten minutes or so, they got back into Jack's car and drove back into the city. They parked behind Jack's apartment building, hugged, and went their separate ways for the night.

Dave felt horny when he headed for his bedroom. Jack was having a definite impact on his mind and body. Lying in bed, Dave jacked off thinking about Jack.

The next day, Jack made the usual drive out to the campus to visit Dave and eat lunch. As they walked, Dave decided to ask Jack a question that was pressing on him.

"Look, would you be interested in going away for the weekend to Atlantic City? We could get a room, gamble if we want to, or just walk the boards. Whaddaya say?"

Jack smiled and stopped. "It's about time you asked me to go away for a couple days. Sure, when do you wanna go?"

"How about next weekend? We could leave on Friday night and come back Sunday afternoon. That sound okay?"

"Yeah, that sounds great. Is this for sure, or do you wanna think about it some more?"

"No, I don't need to think anymore. Let's do it. We'll have to use your car, of course. I hope that's not a problem."

"Nope, no problem at all. It's a date, then," Jack said with a huge smile on his face.

The rest of the day went swiftly as he fantasized about the upcoming weekend. Dave would make all his moves then, and he already hoped that Jack would be more than willing to give him whatever he wanted.

THE following day, Dave decided to talk to Andrew Blankenship about the situation that was fast becoming a problem for him.

"Mr. Blankenship, could I have a couple minutes of your time? It's kinda important."

Blankenship looked at his watch. "How about at two o'clock? I can give you ten minutes then. Will that do?"

"Yes, sir, that'll be fine. See you at two."

It seemed like the clock moved ever so slowly as Dave waited for two o'clock, and he had trouble concentrating on the brief he was reading for court next week. Finally, 1:59 rolled around, and Dave got up to knock on Mr. Blankenship's door.

"Hi, Dave. Come in. What can I do for you?"

"Well, sir, this isn't an easy conversation for me to have, but I feel I have to discuss this issue with you."

"Oh, this doesn't sound good. You're not leaving us, are you?"

"No, sir, it's not that at all. Here's the issue. I met Franklin Venchenzo when I went to the opening of Oz last weekend. While there, he sent me a bottle of champagne, Dom Perignon in fact, and even asked me to dance."

"You danced with Venchenzo? Are you gay, Dave?"

"Ah, yes, sir I am. I had no intention of ever bringing this subject up here at the office, but now I have to."

"Okay, go on."

"The next day, I got a very large and expensive floral arrangement from him at my apartment even though I never told him where I lived. Then he contacted you and hired the firm to represent him so that if I won't see him socially, I will have to because of my job. I sent him a thank you note for the flowers but decided not to go back to the club."

"I see. You think this man is interested in you, and you don't want his attention, is that it?"

"Yes, sir, that's exactly it. I meet this guy one time, and he ends up finding out where I live and work and is making it necessary for me to see him even though I don't want to."

"Forgive me, Dave, if I sound a little ignorant in this area, but I've had very little contact with the gay community and that life. You believe he wants to take you to bed?"

"Yes, but I think he wants far more than that. I think he wants me to become his partner."

"Why would he want you to buy into the club?"

"No, sir, his partner as in *life* partner."

"Ah, I see. What is it that you want me to do?"

"Well, sir, I don't want to have any dealings with him on office business. It's my desire not to have any further contact with him. Is that a problem?"

"Well, it's only a problem if he asks me why I won't send you to him with papers or something. What do I tell him, Dave? Help me out here."

"Could you tell him that I'm tied up on a major case for the firm and you can't afford to interrupt my work to essentially function as a courier?"

Blankenship thought about that for a moment. "Okay, that'll work. I want you to be happy here, and I can see where this would make you very uncomfortable. I'll do what I can."

"Thank you, sir. I really appreciate it. Could you also tell the staff that I'm not to be used for that client?"

"Sure, I'll take care of it at the office staff meeting tomorrow morning."

The meeting ended better than Dave had hoped for, and he was relieved that his being gay had no discernable effect on Mr. Blankenship. Sometimes being desirable was more of a curse than an asset. More and more, Dave began to understand the plight of many women.

Chapter 5

IT WAS Friday night, and Dave was busy packing to go away for the weekend. He was supposed to meet Jack at six p.m. and leave immediately, planning to get something to eat on the road. As he put a carry-on bag down on the floor, he looked around the apartment and made sure the windows were locked. A fire escape ran from the ground outside the living room window all the way to the third floor. Directly outside his window was a landing where people could move around a bit if an emergency required they use it. The good thing about this escape was that as soon as anyone stepped onto it, a metallic rattle sounded out nice and loud. It was almost impossible for anyone to climb the fire escape without Dave knowing.

Satisfied with the apartment security, Dave got his bag and left to wait out front for Jack. A minute later Jack flew out of his apartment building with his own bag, and they headed for Jack's car, which was parked behind the building. They threw the bags into the back seat and left the city en route to Atlantic City.

"I talked with my boss yesterday about Venchenzo. He was completely supportive."

"You told him you're gay, then?"

"Yep, didn't seem to faze him at all. He agreed that I wouldn't have any contact with the guy and that if he asked for me, he would be told that I was tied up on a major case."

"You feel better now?"

"Yeah, more or less. I'm glad we're going away this weekend. I'm looking forward to having some fun."

"My friends warned me not to go with you to AC," Jack said with a sideways glance.

"Huh? Warned you? Why? They're afraid that I'm gonna hurt you or something?"

"No, they're afraid all you want to do is fuck me and leave me for the next guy. They don't wanna see me hurt, that's all."

"Get out! Are you serious?"

"'Fraid so. You have a reputation for fucking a lot of guys and then dumping them. But I chose to ignore them. I'm a big boy."

"That's ridiculous. I haven't dumped anyone. Sure, I've had sex with a couple of guys, but there was never a relationship with anyone to be able to dump them!"

"Did you actually say a *couple* of guys?" Jack laughed loudly. "I like your definition of a couple. I'll have to remember it if I ever gain a *couple* of pounds," he said, laughing once again.

"Your friends aren't being fair to me. They don't know shit about me and are just listening to gossip queens."

"Don't get all defensive. I'm just telling you that I went against the wishes of my friends by going away with you. Do you want to just fuck me and leave me?"

Dave was taken aback by the direct question. "Well, I'm not going to lie to you. I was hoping that if you were into it, that I might enjoy that particular aspect of your tight little body."

Jack laughed again. "That's a fancy way of saying *yeah, I wanna fuck you.* Never knew Marines were so timid."

"Timid! I'll show you timid when we're alone in the room!"

"I'd be lying if I said I wasn't counting on that."

THEY stopped for burgers on the way and made it to Atlantic City just after nine thirty. They checked into one of the motels that stood on the fringe of the downtown area. It was considerably cheaper than the high rise casinos that lined the boardwalk.

When they turned the lights on in the room and looked around, both men were satisfied with what they saw. The room was clean and neat. When Jack jumped onto the bed and bounced, Dave noticed a small box next to the bed on the floor.

"What the hell is that?" Dave asked as he pointed to the box.

Jack leaned over the edge of the bed and looked. He began to laugh. "This is a damn vibrating bed!" Jack rolled around as they laughed at the thought of finding one of these icons of the past still in operation.

Dave pulled out a quarter and put it into the slot. The bed began to vibrate, making Jack laugh all over again. Dave sat down on the bed and smiled. It felt kinda nice, really. When the bed stopped vibrating, Dave picked up the box to look at it closer. When he pushed on the back panel, the back opened up and his quarter fell out.

"Holy shit! We can vibrate all weekend for free!" This cracked both guys up, and the laughing only ended when Jack planted a kiss on Dave's lips.

"Hmm, that was nice," Dave said. When he leaned over to get more, Jack rolled off the bed and opened his bag. He pulled out a bottle of Canadian Club whisky and some snacks. He also moved his toothbrush and stuff into the bathroom.

"It's your job to find ice and mixer. I brought the booze."

"Yes, sir!" Dave said and got up and searched for the ice bucket. The bucket was easier to find than the ice machine. He finally found it to the rear of the motel office. He filled up the bucket and stopped by the desk to get another. Armed with two full buckets of ice, Dave returned to the room.

When he entered, he found Jack lying on the bed with the television on, clad only in a very skimpy pair of black briefs.

"Wow, that's nice looking," Dave said, looking at Jack's junk.

Jack smiled. "Make me a drink."

"Yes, sir," Dave answered. "Unless you want it straight or with water, I better go get the soda. Whaddaya want?"

"Either ginger ale or Coke, please."

"Your wish and all that... I'll be back as soon as I find a place." A few minutes later and Dave was back in the room. He pulled out four bottles of soda, two of each kind. While he was out getting the soda, Jack had hung up what little clothes he had brought with him. He also had taken out a bottle of lube and several condoms and put them on the other side of the lamp next to the bed. Then he had pulled down the covers and climbed into bed. "Now, I take it you want ginger ale with the CC?"

"Yes, please."

Dave smiled and turned back around and made two drinks in the plastic cups he found in the bathroom. They weren't very elegant, but they would do the trick. He carried Jack's drink over to the side of the bed Jack had claimed and brought his drink over to his nightstand.

"I see you're not planning on going out anywhere tonight, since you have your pants and shirt off. So I guess I'll join ya."

Dave found that he was a little self-conscious undressing in front of Jack, who was already in bed. Dave faced the mirror and removed his shirt and shoes and sat down on the bed to take off his socks. He stood up and removed his pants—but not his underwear—and got into bed. They both took sips of their drinks and fluffed the pillows.

Jack watched Dave and smiled but didn't say anything. Dave took the look as the go-ahead for whatever he had in mind. He pulled Jack onto his side facing him and kissed him slowly and gently, taking his time. He rubbed Jack's shoulders as he worked his tongue into Jack's mouth. The kiss lasted well over a minute, and then both put their heads down on the pillows and looked at each other.

"You know, I think there's something special about you," Dave said. "I'm not sure what, but I think that it's the fact that you don't put up a front to people. You are who you are, and you're very comfortable with yourself. You're a caring person, which I like very much. I don't think there's a violent bone in your body, am I right?"

"Yes to all the above. I don't like violence and would prefer to make love," Jack said coyly. "I'm also very turned on by you and think you're a pretty cool guy."

Dave leaned over and kissed Jack more passionately the second time. He ran his hands through Jack's hair as he pulled him partially on top of him. He ran his hands down Jack's back and back up his sides. He began to plant little kisses all over Jack's neck and then pulled him over so that Jack was now on the opposite side of the bed. He continued to kiss Jack and mingle tongues with him.

Dave's fingers began to travel and found Jack's nipples, tweaking them and rubbing them until they were hard. Dave flicked his tongue over each of them, eliciting a low groan from Jack. As he sucked on one nipple, he let his hand coast down Jack's chest and continue toward Jack's cock, expecting to find underwear. When his hand hit pubic hair and then an erection, Dave looked up and said, "Well, you dirty dog, you've been waiting on me to make my move, eh?"

"If you think I came all the way to Atlantic City to look at the water, you've got the wrong guy in bed with you," Jack said with a smile.

"Wow, that's quite a surprise in my hand," Dave said as he moved his hand over the entire area. "I think I need to see it."

Dave threw the covers off Jack and found, to his immense joy, a rather well-endowed bedmate. He moved his hand back over Jack's cock and down onto his balls, fondling them gently. "Boy, am I gonna have fun with these," he said.

"Well stop talking and start the fun!"

"With pleasure."

Dave slid down in the bed until he was even with Jack's cock. Jack was on the large size, but not so large that Dave couldn't do whatever he wanted. He shifted over between Jack's legs and saw that his balls were hanging down almost to the sheets. He pulled Jack's cock toward his mouth and began to lick the head of his dick. He swirled his tongue around the opening as well as the ridge around the head. He then slid his tongue down Jack's shaft until he hit balls, where he allowed his tongue to travel over both at the same time. He gently took each ball on his tongue and rolled it around before letting each drop from his mouth. He worked his way back up to Jack's cock and began to go up and down on it, slowly picking up speed.

He was unable to get all of it into his mouth and used a hand on that part of the shaft he couldn't suck. Jack's legs began to move around, and Dave got the hint that he was going too fast. He eased off and let Jack's cock fall out of his mouth. Kissing his way back up Jack's body, Dave stopped at his mouth, where he kissed Jack long and hard once again. After several minutes of kissing, Dave pulled away from Jack and grabbed his drink.

"This is thirsty work here," he said with a smile.

Jack took a sip of his own drink and said, "Don't you think it's time we had the unveiling of the rest of your body?"

Dave smiled and replied, "Of course, my dear." He kicked off his briefs, allowing his own erection to spring loose and point toward the headboard of the bed. Jack smiled. Apparently he liked what he saw very much.

"Just right. Not too big and not too small."

"For what?" Dave asked.

"For fucking," Jack replied.

"Who says I wanna fuck you?"

"Oh please! All of Reading knows you wanna fuck me!"

When Dave stopped laughing, he put his hand on Jack's chest and asked, "What positions do you like the best?"

"Hell if I know. I'm a virgin."

"Huh?"

"You heard me. I've never been fucked before. You think everyone is a wanton hussy like you?"

"I'm gonna get to pop your cherry! I love it, and I promise to be gentle. You'll see."

"You better be, or it will be the only time you get this ass."

They finished their first drinks, and Dave asked Jack to make them another one. As Jack took the cups and got out of bed, Dave got his first look at Jack's ass. What he saw made him rock hard, and he almost begin to pant.

"You've got a beautiful ass on you, dude!"

Jack turned his head and looked back over his shoulder and replied, "You like it, then?"

"Damn right I like it. It's a thing of beauty. What do you do, ass exercises?"

"Yep. We got to take care of the assets we have, don't we?"

"Incredible. I can't wait to tap that."

"Tap that, oh, how romantic!" Jack replied.

"Oh, I'm sorry. I don't mean to be crude or anything, but damn!"

Jack laughed and said it was fine. He handed Dave his second drink, which Dave put down immediately, and as Jack climbed into bed, Dave's hands were all over him.

"Damn, dude, I want you so bad."

"So, you didn't want me before you saw my ass, then?"

"Ha ha, you know I did."

"Then show me."

That was all Dave needed to hear. He moved in for a kiss and held it for a long time. He then lay back and pulled Jack's head down onto his chest, and Jack took it from there. Jack began to kiss Dave's nipples and lightly nibble on each, sending shockwaves of pleasure through Dave. Jack then slid down Dave's body quickly, leaving one set of fingers on each nipple as he took Dave's cock into his mouth and began to suck.

Dave had already begun to leak, and he enjoyed the heat of Jack's mouth as Jack took Dave's entire cock in until the head hit the back of his throat. Dave pushed his head back into the pillows as the sensations overwhelmed him. Dave grabbed Jack's head and held it still as he begun to thrust into Jack's willing mouth. Dave's head thrashed from side to side as he continued to pump between Jack's lips. Finally, he pulled out and guided Jack down onto his balls.

Jack worked Dave's balls over with his tongue and mouth. He brought one hand down and began to jerk Dave's cock as he licked them. He continued to jerk Dave as he took the head of his dick into his mouth and sucked. Dave wrapped his legs around Jack's back and cried out, "Yeah, suck it! Suck it good!"

Keeping his legs wrapped around Jack, Dave rolled him over so that he was thrusting downward into Jack's mouth. As Dave fucked Jack's mouth, Jack played with Dave's ass and balls. When Dave began to enjoy the sex a little too much, he quickly untangled himself from Jack and switched positions so that Jack was back on top.

Jack took the hint, and he began to fuck Dave's mouth harder and deeper than Dave had done to him. Dave actually had to time his breathing just right so that he could breathe on the out strokes, because Jack went deep enough that he cut off Dave's air. As Dave watched Jack thrust in and out, he saw Jack's balls begin to climb toward the base of his cock, and he knew that if Jack didn't stop soon, he would be drowning in Jack's essence.

As if Jack was reading Dave's mind, he suddenly pulled out, climbed off of Dave, and lay on his back, breathing heavily. Dave swallowed and got his breath back before taking the next step.

"Can I have your ass?"

Jack looked at Dave and said, "Yes, but remember your promise to be gentle."

"Have no fear of that at all. I intend to make many return visits to your beautiful body, and the last thing I want to do is hurt you."

Jack reached around the lamp and retrieved the rubbers and lube, putting them down on the bed between them. Dave smiled and said, "You've thought ahead. Were you that sure I would succumb to your charms and wanna fuck you?"

"Oh please, there are only two reasons to come to Atlantic City: to gamble and to fuck. Do you see us at a table somewhere?"

"No, I guess you're right," Dave said with a smile.

Dave coated two fingers with lube and slid farther down on the bed. He reached under Jack's leg and probed between his ass cheeks until he found the rosebud and began to coat it. As he massaged the lube into the opening, he slowly worked one finger into the tight orifice. Once it was all the way in, Dave finger-fucked Jack until he worked a second finger in. He turned his fingers around in the opening, trying to stretch the muscle so that it could accommodate his cock.

When he felt Jack was relaxed enough and was enjoying the stimulation he was receiving, Dave slipped a condom on his cock and coated it liberally with lube. He added more to his fingers and slipped one inside to leave behind more lube and then got up on his knees between Jack's.

"Now just relax and remember to breathe. The key is to not tighten up. It may hurt at first, but the pain will pass, and then you'll begin to enjoy it. My hope is that you'll love it and will want it time and time again," Dave said with a smile.

"Okay. Just stop if I say stop, okay?"

"Absolutely. You can trust me in this. Believe me."

"Is that like 'I promise I won't come in your mouth'?" Jack asked.

"Ha ha, no. Here we go."

Dave moved forward and guided his cock with one hand until he found the opening. He then pressed in slightly to keep his dick lined up correctly.

"Now relax…."

Dave pushed a little farther, and when there was no protest, he pushed until he felt himself pop through the ring of resistance.

"Ah, that hurts, stop!"

"Okay, okay, I won't go in any farther. Just relax. It'll stop hurting."

Jack had a hand on each of Dave's legs and was pushing back with both. When Dave felt the pressure fade, he began to push farther into Jack.

"You're doing incredible. I'm almost all the way in."

"I'm okay. Just go slowly. I feel full now."

"Yeah, you will. That's the pressure inside from my cock coming in."

When Dave hit bottom, he said, "There, I'm all the way in… just stay relaxed."

After waiting for a minute, Jack said, "Okay, I'm feeling all right."

Dave began to gently and slowly rock in and out, making sure that he didn't come all the way out. As he pushed back in, he felt Jack begin to relax, and Dave knew that he would be fine. As Dave picked up the speed, Jack began to smile as Dave looked down into his blue eyes.

"You're beautiful. You know that, right?" Dave asked as he thrust in and out. Jack smiled but didn't reply, jerking his own cock while he was getting fucked. "That's it. You're doing fantastic. This feels so fucking good my toes are curling."

"I'm getting into it as well. You keep hitting a spot that feels real good, almost like little bolts of electricity."

"Yeah, that would be your prostate that I'm hitting. It's the male G-spot."

Dave now increased to normal speed on his thrusts, and it wasn't too long before he felt his climax begin to build. As he looked down into Jack's eyes, he felt the tsunami of his orgasm build and finally explode as he let out a moan that sent shivers through both men. As Dave finished shooting, Jack began to come. His muscles tightened like a ring of steel around Dave's softening cock, squeezing out any fluid that was left. When Jack finished, Dave collapsed onto Jack's chest as they both began to drift down from their climaxes. Dave raised his head far enough to kiss Jack on the lips and whisper, "That was great!"

After a minute or so, Dave's dick popped out of Jack's ass, and he rolled off him. Jack quickly got up and went into the bathroom where he took a washcloth and wet it with hot water. Dave watched Jack clean himself off, rinse the cloth, and bring it out to the bed with him. He wiped Dave's body down, including his cock after Dave removed the used condom.

Jack returned the washcloth to the sink, where he rinsed it out again and then draped it over a towel rack on the back of the door. He refilled their drinks and rejoined Dave in bed.

"That was fucking fantastic, dude. I swear there is nothing like popping a guy for the first time. It's not only special, but it seems to be the ultimate in anal sex. I hope you enjoyed it," Dave said as he looked at Jack.

"Yeah, I liked it very much. You took your time like you promised and were very gentle. In fact, toward the end there, you could've rocked it, I was into it so much."

Dave smiled and said, "I'll remember that for the next time."

They lay in bed, sipping their drinks and talking for a couple more hours before they became tired enough to sleep. When that time arrived, Jack turned off the lights, and they fell asleep in each other's arms, totally satisfied.

Chapter 6

THEY woke up a little after nine the next morning, and Dave turned on his side to look into Jack's eyes. He smiled, remembering last night, and then pulled the covers down. Since Jack was lying on his stomach, his bare ass was exposed to Dave's hungry eyes.

"Damn, I could get use to waking up to that every morning," he said as he ran his hand over the curve of Jack's ass. He slowly caressed the object of his renewed desire and became hard, which Jack noticed at once.

"You can have a second go at it if you like," he said with a lazy smile as he stretched.

"That's exactly what I had in mind, actually," Dave replied.

"I could tell by looking at your dick."

Dave reached over Jack, grabbed the lube and condoms, and once again began the preparation routine that would allow Dave to experience the joy of fucking Jack once more. Once Jack was ready, Dave slipped on the condom, lubed up his erection, and left Jack face down in the pillows. He was mounting Jack in the good, old-fashioned way so that he could drive his cock down into Jack at whatever pace he desired.

As he slowly slipped his cock into Jack, Jack let out a soft moan that was a cross between desire and fulfillment. When Dave's balls were resting on Jack's ass, he bent his head down and kissed Jack on the nape of the neck. Jack turned his face as far around as he could, meeting Dave the rest of the way and kissing him on the lips.

"This feels so fucking good," Dave said as he began to move in and out.

"Hmm, you're telling me. I've been missing something all my life."

Dave picked up speed, quicker than he had before, and was beginning to pound down into Jack with gusto. Jack groaned louder—Dave knew it was the thrusting once again creating the unfamiliar feel of his prostate being rubbed repeatedly. The repeated thrusts also rocked Jack's body forward and backward on his now-hard cock, creating a masturbatory effect.

Dave became lost in the driving of his cock, and he hardly heard the resounding smack of their bodies each time he completed a downward thrust. Not only was Jack rocking, but the bed began to move with the motion as well.

Finally, Dave began to feel his orgasm build, and he didn't even think once about slowing down to prolong it. He pounded all the harder. "Shit, I'm gonna come!" he said through clenched teeth.

"Give it to me, stud! I'm loving it!" Jack replied.

After another dozen thrusts, Dave was filling the condom once more. His pace of thrusting began to slow down as the climax ebbed until he stopped and collapsed on Jack's back. Breathing heavily, Dave lay there enjoying the intense feelings. Somehow it felt so right, so much more than just sex.

"Fuck, that was incredible, guy," Dave whispered and kissed Jack's neck.

"Hmmm, felt good," was the only response from a smiling Jack.

Dave pulled out, took off the condom, and fell back onto the bed, where he stared at the ceiling wondering what it meant that this particular fuck seemed to mean more than they usually did. Was this more like making love than merely fucking? Was this the man he was destined to meet and fall in love with?

Jack snuggled into Dave's side and gave a contented sigh. He put one arm over Dave's chest and kissed Dave's arm. They fell asleep once more and only woke up when housekeeping knocked on the door.

Dave jumped out of bed and threw on a pair of sweatpants as Jack pulled the sheets up over himself. Dave ran to the door, cracked it opened, and was greeted by not one, but two cleaning ladies.

"Ah, can you skip us today? We're kinda lying in."

"Yes, no problem. Do you want fresh towels," she asked, holding out an arm full of linens.

"Sure, we'll take them. Thank you."

He closed the door and went into the bathroom where he set them down on the counter.

"Are we going to stay in bed all day or are you hungry, buttercup?" Dave asked.

"Who the fuck is 'buttercup'?" Jack asked with a laugh.

"You are," Dave responded as he jumped onto the bed, pulled the covers back, and kissed Jack squarely on the ass.

Jack wiggled his ass in response and began laughing. "You're too much," he said.

"I've been told that once or twice."

"Hey, I'm beginning to feel a little sore after that pounding you just gave me! You damage the merchandise, you buy it," Jack warned.

"Hmm, I might buy it damaged or not!"

Dave went into the bathroom, turned on the shower, and climbed in. Jack was right behind him and together they washed each other in all the right places. Dave paid extensive attention to Jack's cock and made sure it was *very* clean.

After twenty minutes, they got out, dried off, and got dressed. It was time to go find breakfast. As they left the room, Dave dropped off the used towels and washcloth with the cleaning ladies, and they continued on through the streets until they saw the Atlantic Ocean. It was a beautiful day, and they walked about half a mile along the boardwalk before choosing one of the casino hotels for breakfast.

After breakfast, they toured a couple casinos, dropping a few quarters into the slots, winning exactly one dollar more than they put into the bandits. As they headed back to the motel, Dave was thankful that the Jersey Shore existed, and he knew he and Jack would be back again.

The rest of the weekend was spent the way it began, and by the time they left on Sunday, Jack was definitely no longer a virgin in any respect. The ride home was peaceful, and both men were happy that they'd spent the weekend together.

"You know, Jack, I think you're pretty cool. You know that, right?"

"I'm into you too. You wanna date and see where this goes?"

"For sure, dude. That means you cut Billy off from your dick—no more blow jobs from him, right?"

"Yeah, okay. What do I do if I have to leave that apartment?"

"You fucking move in with me, that's what you do."

"Okay, let's see how it all plays out."

THE week went by normally, including seeing Jack on campus on Wednesday. On Thursday morning, Mr. Blankenship called Dave into his office. Dave figured it was because of Venchenzo and that it wasn't going to be good news.

"Hi, Dave, thanks for stopping by. Look, this matter with the Club Oz and its owner, Franklin Venchenzo, has come up again. He has asked us to handle some real estate transactions for him up in the Pocono Mountains, and he's insisting that you be the one to handle all the paperwork, including taking a trip with him to the region. He wants to look at the properties one more time before we handle the contracts and closings, and he thinks it will be an overnight trip. I know how you feel, and I wanted to ask you if you would consider doing this one time for the firm."

Dave was shocked. He forced down the bolt of anger that shot throughout his body before answering his boss. "Mr. Blankenship, I thought I made it plain, but if I didn't, let me do so now. This guy wants me in his bed. He's using this firm as his pimp to make that happen since I won't go to him on my own. Are you honestly telling me that you would pimp me out to retain him as a client? Is that what I mean to you and the other partners?"

"Well, you are gay after all. I'm sure you've done this sort of thing many times before, right?"

Dave stood and leaned on the front edge of the desk. "Let me make sure you understand my answer: No! Under no circumstances will I interact in any way with this guy. I for sure am not sleeping with him for your profit margin. And one more thing: just because I'm gay does *not* mean that I'll sleep with just anyone. Any questions?" Dave asked angrily.

"Calm down, first of all. I have to be honest with you. Times are tight right now, and we need clients like Franklin Venchenzo to keep the bottom line of the firm in the black. Won't you reconsider your decision in this matter? There would be a sizable bonus in it for you."

"Bonus? Are you kidding me? First you want me just to whore myself out for the firm, now you're suggesting maybe I would rather be a prostitute? The answer is no!"

"Very well, Dave. I understand. Thank you."

Dave left the office and returned to his desk under a full head of steam. He hadn't been this angry since two of his buddies got him shitfaced drunk so they could try and fuck him. As he sat at his desk, he thought about quitting the firm. Did he really want to work for someone who would use him for sexual purposes to keep business? If he quit, where would he work next? Dave was sure if he quit that he would be blackballed in the Reading legal community.

He picked up the phone and called Jack. "Hey, you busy?"

"Hi, Dave. Not really, I'm on my break. What's up?"

"What are you doing for lunch?"

"Brown bag is in my drawer, why?"

"Fuck that. Meet me at the diner at 5th and Penn. I need to talk to you."

"Sounds serious. Okay, say twelve fifteen?"

"Yeah, that works. If you get there first, grab a table."

Dave hung up the phone and tried to go over his options. Should he just give in and put out once? The thought of letting this guy fuck him made Dave feel like throwing up. If he did give in, would that just make Venchenzo a permanent nightmare?

Susan the office manager came up to Dave and sat down.

"The partners need the yearly financial projections by the end of the day. Can you meet that deadline?"

"I'll certainly try. But I have to go out for lunch. I'm meeting someone."

"Are you sure that's wise? It could be your job if you're late with the projections."

"I'll just have to take that risk."

"Okay, let me know when you've finished so that I can let them know."

Dave watch Susan walked away and knew that this was the first bit of subtle pressure being applied by Blankenship to get him to change his mind regarding Venchenzo. It wasn't going to work.

He looked at his watch and saw that he had ten minutes to get to the diner, so he left the office. Anger began to build in Dave once more as he thought about Venchenzo becoming a major distraction in his life. He knew he couldn't just go to the club and tell the guy to fuck off. The muscle that hung around the club would no doubt prevent any unpleasantness from occurring, and Venchenzo had already demonstrated that he might not be the type of man it was wise to confront.

As he walked into the diner, Jack waved from a table in the back. Dave smiled as he approached the table. Just seeing Jack released some of the pressure. It was a combination of the blond hair, blue eyes, and the smile that was just for him.

"Hey, thanks for meeting me. Lunch is on me," Dave said.

"No problem. Let's order, and then tell me what's going on."

When the waitress walked away from the table, Dave put his face in his hands and sighed. "Look, this clown Venchenzo is now a major problem. He has the firm almost demanding that I sleep with the guy just so they can keep his business. Venchenzo wants me to go to the Poconos with him for an overnight to inspect some property that he wants to buy."

"No way! Are you serious? How in the hell do they think they can get away with asking you to do that?"

"Not only that, but they are already putting pressure on me to change my mind. I have a project due by the end of the day that I originally had until the end of next week to finish. Frankly, I don't know what to do."

"Well, you're not going to sleep with this guy, I hope!"

"Would that upset you?"

"Upset me? Are you shitting me? Of course it would upset me. Damn it, Dave. I have feelings for you, in case that fact escaped your sex-starved consciousness. You can't do it," Jack exclaimed.

"You have feelings for me?"

"Ah, yeah, I do. I wasn't going to mention it at all, but it slipped out with this crap hitting me. Didn't you say you slept with a Reading cop among the thousands of men you've conquered?"

"What kind of feelings?"

"I don't know. *Feelings*, damn it! Answer my question."

They stopped talking as the food was placed on the table and coffee poured.

"Yeah, I did sleep with a cop… and it hasn't been thousands. At most it's mere hundreds!"

"Talk to him as soon as you can. This has to be alleviated somehow, but I gotta tell you something first. If this gets out, I'll lose my job and I could even be prosecuted for what I'm about to tell you. I wasn't intending to tell you, as you know, but this has become far too serious," Jack said, clearly worried. "When I checked the records, I found all kinds of connections to northern New Jersey. He has bank accounts of over five million dollars that he can draw from. He's a major player, and if I had to guess, I would think organized crime. When you told me about Louie and friends, it kinda made everything come together."

Dave sat back in his chair and chewed on a bite of his hamburger. When he swallowed, he replied, "Great. That's just great. So, not only could I lose my job over this clown, but you're telling me that I could end up off the Jersey coast sleeping with the fishes? Nice. I thought they didn't like gay members?"

"When they're moneymakers like this guy seems to be, the Mob tends to overlook things. We can always move away, you know."

"You'd move away from Reading for me?"

"Yes."

"I don't know what to say."

"Then don't say anything. Just keep it in the back of your mind as an option… and don't give into this guy."

THEY finished lunch and went back to their offices. Dave put a call into Derrick at the city police department. He was told that Derrick was on the road and that Dave's message would be given to him when he came back in since it wasn't an emergency.

Dave hung up, turned to his computer, and brought up the file he had to finish by five. Two hours later, Derrick phoned.

"Thanks for returning my call," Dave said. "I've got a problem that I need your professional advice on, and it's kinda serious. Do you have some time for me maybe tonight?"

"Are you in some kind of trouble?"

"Not the kind you're thinking of, no, but it could become a police situation."

"What time do you get off?"

"I'm off at five."

"Okay, I take it you don't want me to come into your place of employment, correct?"

"That would be a big yes. I don't want you near my place of employment."

"Okay, why don't I stop by your apartment around five thirty? I'll still be on duty, but that isn't a problem."

"That would be fantastic of you. Thank you so much."

"Okay, see you then."

Dave felt much better when he hung up. He still had a lot of work to do on the projections so he wasted no time in getting back to work.

At 4:47, Dave finished the financial report and handed it over to the office manager who was waiting by her desk.

"I didn't think you'd be able to get this done. Are you sure the data is correct?"

"Yes, the data is correct. Anything else this afternoon?"

"No, nothing."

"Why did the due date on this move up to today? It wasn't due until the end of next week. Did Blankenship ask you for it?"

"Yes, Mr. Blankenship said there was an urgent need for the data and asked to have it today. Was that a problem for you?"

"No, as you can see the report is done," Dave replied.

"Then you have a good night."

Dave left the office feeling good. He had gotten the report in and eliminated an excuse for the firm to fire him. He walked quickly up Penn Street, looking over his shoulder every once in a while. He arrived at his apartment at five fifteen and ran up the stairs to open some windows and let fresh air into the apartment. He poured himself some soda and waited for the door bell to ring.

Exactly at five thirty, Derrick arrived. Dave let him into the apartment, and they sat down. Dave explained the entire problem to Derrick and then asked what he thought he should do.

"Well, this is a new one on me: a gay mobster running a gay club in Reading. Actually, now that I think of it, it's really not that out of sync for the city. Look, Reading has a very long history of Mob connections and official corruption going back to the early days of Prohibition. Hell, Bugsy Siegel owned the apartment building two doors down from this very location. When he was in Reading, he stayed in that house, which back then was one house and not apartments. Reading also used to be the home of illegal slot machines and the money from that controlled the political establishment and the police force. Now, it's more drugs than anything else, but with the drugs has come increased violence. So, I'm not sure which crime era is or was better for Reading."

"I had no idea. Here I thought Reading was just a nice little city that grew with the area. Now you tell me this was like a little Chicago."

"Yep, and except for the type of crime, it's almost the same. Corruption in City Hall is nowhere what it used to be, but I'm sure someone is on the payroll for someone. I'm sure the police bosses know who this Venchenzo is, but word hasn't reached down to my level yet. What do you want me to do?"

"I'm not sure. He hasn't really done anything illegal toward me. Right now, the worst he could be accused of is buying me champagne at the club that he owns. Should I meet with him and tell him to back off? Or will that get me hurt?"

"Depends on how you do it. Remember, respect is a big thing with these guys. You go in there and call him a troll or something, and yeah, you're probably gonna get a payback. Do it right, and he might be okay with it. The guy who's really on thin ice is your boss. What he asked violates labor laws. You might wanna look for another job."

"Yeah, that's an idea. The direct pressure is coming from my boss and not Venchenzo. I also don't want anyone I care about getting hurt."

"Is there someone you care about?"

"Yeah, I think so. Just spent the weekend with him in Atlantic City."

"So, I guess that means we won't be having a repeat of our date, then?" Derrick asked with a frown.

"I had a great time with you, Derrick, and you're a great guy who's fantastic in bed. But I think I might have found the guy for me."

"That's cool. I understand. I hope he knows how lucky he is to have you."

"I think *I'm* the lucky one! And as hot as you are, you'll have no problem finding more guys that want nothing more than to bed you, and that doesn't even bring up the fact that you're a cop. What red-blooded gay boy doesn't want to make love to a cop?"

"Look, why don't you do this: You and I go in there together and have dinner. While I'm there, you go and talk with this guy and tell him politely that you're not interested. This way, I'm in the dining room and will expect you to come back. If you don't come back, I'll go looking for you."

"That would be incredible! Look, I'm no baby, and I've looked danger in the eye more than once as a Marine, but this… this is something altogether different. I don't feel like I'm on an even playing field with Venchenzo."

"When would you like to do this?"

"When are you off next?"

"I'm rotating shifts tomorrow, so I'll be off for the next three days."

"Okay, I'm buying you dinner at Oz Saturday night. Will that work?"

"Yep, that's fine. I'll come here, and then we'll go together. In the meantime, you work out the little speech you're gonna give the man. Remember, be respectful."

"Okay, I feel a lot better now with a plan. Once he's taken care of, I'll take care of my boss. I don't know how I'm ever going to be able to repay you for doing this."

Derrick raised an eyebrow and said, "Oh, I can think of a way if you want a suggestion."

"Damn, you're as big a horndog as I am!"

THE next day at work, Blankenship was in court all day, much to Dave's relief. He managed to get through the day without seeing him once. Dave left the office, and as he was about to enter his apartment building, Jack was just getting home from work.

"Hey, guy, how was your day?" Dave asked.

"Not bad. What about you?"

"The evil boss was in court all day so I didn't have to interact with him at all. You wanna come for dinner at my place tonight? I'll cook and you eat. How's that sound?"

"I'd love to come for dinner. I'll bring a bottle of wine. What time?"

"Say about seven?"

"See you in a couple hours, then!"

DAVE ran up the stairs and went into his apartment in a very happy mood. This would be the first time he cooked for Jack, and he wanted to make sure the food tasted good. When he checked his refrigerator, though, he found that he lacked any inspiration for something to make. He sat down at the table and tried to think of something to create, and when he couldn't, he decided to cheat.

He picked up the phone and dialed a local restaurant that the law firm represented and ordered two dinners to go. He would pick up the food, make sure it stayed warm, and serve it on dinnerware when Jack came over. He made sure to order something simple but tasty and knew Jack would love it.

When he got back from the restaurant, he unpacked the food and took the chicken marsala, pasta with butter and cheese, and fresh green beans and placed it all in warming pans to put in the oven. He decided to make a salad and pulled out the ingredients, chopping everything up and combining it all in a big bowl. He set the table and made sure the temperature wasn't too high on the oven.

Then he jumped into the shower, shaved, and got dressed. He had just enough time to sit down with a drink and relax afterward. Maybe it was also time to invite Jack to spend the night as well? He jumped up, ran into the bedroom, stripped the sheets and pillowcases off the bed and put fresh linens on. He straightened up his bedroom, made sure he had lube and condoms, and went back to the living room where he finished his drink.

The doorbell rang about seven, and Dave went down to get the door. Jack looked very desirable in his jeans and polo shirt, and Dave knew that Jack was trying to look sexy. He was also wearing one of Dave's favorite colognes. When they entered the apartment, Jack sniffed the air like a Scottish terrier on the scent.

"That smells marvelous! If it tastes half as good as it smells, dinner will be a success," he said as he handed Dave a bottle of wine.

"Are you hungry? If so, we can eat right away. It's ready."

"Yeah, I am kinda hungry, especially after smelling that."

"Great, let's eat," Dave said crossing his fingers that Jack would like the food.

They entered the eat-in kitchen, and Jack sat down at the table. Dave popped the wine and poured each of them a glass. He sipped a little and smiled. "Nice. It should go very well with dinner."

"What is for dinner? I'm dying to know."

"Nothing much. I threw together a little supper of medallions of chicken marsala, penne pasta, and green beans. We also have a salad with some French bread and butter available."

"You're kidding? You made this for me?" Jack asked as he looked at the food being placed on the table.

"Of course! Nothing is too much trouble for you, dude. I hope you like it. Now help yourself."

After tasting the first bite of the chicken, Jack looked at Dave and said, "This is marvelous! I had no idea you could cook like this. Here I'm the chef, and you're whipping up a dinner like this!"

"You're a chef? You mean you know how to cook?" Dave asked with surprise.

"Well, yes, I know how to cook, but that's because I graduated from the Culinary Institute of America. This is damn good!"

"Good, I'm glad you like it."

"I have to ask. How much olive oil did you put into the dish?"

"Ah, olive oil?"

"Yeah, you *did* put in olive oil, right?"

"Oh yeah, of course. I put in about a quarter cup. Can you taste it?"

"Oh yes, I taste it just fine. In fact, the penne and beans are terrific too. Just the right amount of garlic in the beans. How much did you use?"

"Ah, garlic, yes... I think I put two balls in."

"Two balls? What size would that be?"

"You know, two of the garlic things."

"You mean you put two whole heads in?"

"Yeah, that's it. Two heads of garlic."

Jack smiled and put some more on his plate, and they chatted throughout the rest of the dinner.

"I'm stuffed. I hope you didn't make dessert, because I couldn't possibly eat any," Jack said as he patted his stomach.

"No, I didn't think about dessert. Glad you don't want any," Dave said with a laugh. The wine was ideal and finished off the dinner perfectly.

"The dinner was very good. Now will you tell me who made it?"

"Whaddaya mean who made it? I already told you I made it."

"Well, see, it's like this. For this amount of chicken, you would put about four tablespoons of olive oil in the pan, not a quarter cup. As for the garlic, it would have been hard to eat with two whole heads. The normal amount would be around two tablespoons, give or take a teaspoon's worth. And finally, it tastes remarkably like the fine chicken marsala that Jean Pierre's serves over on 13th Street."

"Ahh, damn it, you got me! I did get it from Jean Pierre's. I looked in the refrigerator when I got home and nothing inspired me. I knew you liked good food, so I called up the restaurant and ordered dinner, and I went and picked it up," Dave said as he blushed.

When Jack stopped laughing, he said, "It was truly first rate, and I appreciate very much that you went through all that trouble to fix dinner for me."

"Ah, the salad was all me!"

"And truly a fine salad it was. I liked the variety of ingredients that you used. It really was a wonderful dinner. Maybe you would allow me to make you dinner one night?"

"Sure, I'd love that," Dave said with a smile. "What restaurant are you going to use?"

"Let me help you clear the dishes. It's the least I can do after all this trouble," Jack replied, totally ignoring the question.

"Absolutely not! You just pour yourself something to drink and take it into the living room, and I'll be there shortly. Guests do not clear tables in my house. Now go!"

"I love it when you get so forceful."

"Get or I'll spank you!"

"I hope you mean it," Jack said as he fixed an after-dinner drink and headed down the hallway.

As the night wore on and it became late, Jack stifled a yawn. It had been a work day, and Dave could see he was getting tired. Seeing his opening, Dave took advantage of it. "Look, you're getting tired, and there's really no reason for you to go home this late. Why don't you spend the night? I'll make you breakfast in the morning."

"I don't know... Billy is likely to get lonely if I'm not there again tonight."

"What? I don't give a flying fuck what Billy feels! Fuck Billy!"

Jack broke out laughing and stopped after a few seconds. "I'm busting your balls. Sure, I'd love to spend the night, but I warn you, I *am* tired. It's been a long week."

"That's fine, my dear. Would you like anything to take with you to the bedroom?"

"Nah, I've had enough to drink for one night."

Dave got up and made sure everything was locked up before he turned out the lights. They walked down the hallway to the bedroom with Jack making a detour to the bathroom. Dave lit a candle next to the bed and shut off the rest of the lights, and he closed the curtains so that the morning sun wouldn't wake them before they were ready to get up.

Dave was taking his shirt off when Jack walked into the bedroom, and they smiled at each other. Before too much longer, both men were naked and climbing into bed. They snuggled together after a kiss and sank back into the pillows. Jack placed his head on Dave's chest and kissed the skin surrounding a nipple.

"This is nice. I could get used to it, I think," Dave whispered.

Jack kissed him on the chest again and turned over so that he was looking up at Dave. "Are you trying to tell me something?" Jack asked.

Dave looked at the ceiling and then back at Jack. "Look, I really have a fondness for you, dude, and I think I'm falling in love. It doesn't really make sense for you to keep living in that apartment with the creep while I'm over here wanting you and all alone. Would you consider moving in?"

"Hmm, are we a pair of lesbians?"

"Huh? Whaddaya mean?"

"Lesbians usually have two dates. The first is when they meet and fuck, and the second is packing the U-Haul."

Dave laughed loudly and pulled Jack's head up to his mouth and kissed him. "I think we've had more than two dates. Do you like me? I know you find me hot, but do you like me?"

"Yeah, I do," Jack said. "In fact, it's a little more than like. Besides, I wanna prove my friends wrong."

"Your friends?"

"Yeah, remember? They warned me that all you wanted to do was fuck me and leave me. If I move in, that shoots that warning all to hell!"

"You know, I love proving people wrong. Whaddaya say?"

"What about that creep at Oz?"

"I'm going to take care of that tomorrow night. I'm having dinner there with Derrick, the city cop. I'm gonna talk to Venchenzo, and if I happen to not come back, he'll call in the troops. Either we clear this up, or we'll know that I have a major problem to deal with."

"Okay, just please be careful. I don't want you getting hurt." Jack kissed Dave's chest again. "Promise me?" he continued.

"Yes, dear. Once this is resolved, we'll get you moved in here. If Billy has a problem with it, I'll deal with his ass." Dave then kissed Jack on the lips, clearly communicating "I want to get laid."

"Honey, do you mind if you take your wanton pleasures in the morning? I'm so damn tired, and the wine has really put me in the mood to go to sleep right here on your beautiful chest. It's like sleeping in the mountains," Jack said with a smile.

"You bet. I've got one question for you before we go to sleep, though."

"Yeah?" Jack responded.

"Will you be my lover?"

Jack answered by kissing Dave on the lips and then both pecs. Dave had the answer he had been hoping Jack would give him. Dave turned his head aside and blew out the candle before Jack noticed a tear slip from his right eye. This was what he had always wanted, and it made him think back to when he was in the Marine Corps.

One night, when he was having a rare intimate episode with another Marine who was supposedly straight, he'd kissed the guy on the chest, and his buddy had responded by saying, "Hell, Dave, all you need is someone to love."

The Marine was right and Dave knew it at the time he said it. After all this time, maybe he finally had that. Dave sighed in contentment and said a silent prayer of thanksgiving that he might have found love and a good man to share it with. He kissed Jack on the forehead as Jack began to snore lightly, closed his eyes, and went to sleep filled with a sense of joy.

Chapter 7

THE next morning, Dave and Jack woke up fully rested and horny. Morning wood was very convenient for getting the action started. They took their time and made love, with Dave making sure that he was extra sensitive to Jack's needs. He was overcome with the urge to protect and make this man happy as much as he could.

When they finished, they took a shower together, and when they had dried off, Dave told Jack he was going to "make" breakfast as promised. "You know what? Let's go out for breakfast. About time Reading saw me with you on a regular basis. I'm paying; no argument."

"Yes, sir, no argument, sir!"

Dave slapped Jack on his bare ass, and they ran into the bedroom to get dressed and go out. By the time they got to the restaurant, it was closer to lunchtime, and they switched their appetites away from French toast toward burgers and fries. They took their time, eating and giggling like a couple of kids in love for the first time. Dave was falling hard for this man and knew it. It made him all the more determined to solve the most pressing issue of all—Venchenzo—as soon as possible. He was so happy that he might have found what he had been looking for, believing that only a rare few found true happiness in love. Jack was hot as hell to look at, great in bed, and had a wonderful personality. He was hitting the trifecta with Jack and he knew it.

When they got back to the apartment building, they stood outside for a few moments. "Why don't you start to pack some things. You know, begin to get ready for the move," Dave suggested.

"Yeah, I suppose I could do that. It will take me some time to sort out my stuff from Billy's and find boxes. Guess I can go to the store and get some," Jack replied.

"Okay, and if you have any problems whatsoever from Billy, you tell me right away, and I'll handle him. Okay?"

"Yeah, but you do know I'm a big boy and can take care of things like this, right?"

"Of course I know that, honey, but I don't want you being stressed out by this clown, that's all."

"Okay, I'll give ya a call later. Be careful tonight. You hear, tough guy?" Jack said.

After watching Jack go up the stairs to his building, Dave walked away with a smile. He went upstairs to his apartment and walked around, picturing the changes he needed to make so it would be comfortable for two people instead of just one. The apartment was big enough for three or four, but it was set up just for Dave at this point. He would make room anywhere for anything his Jack wanted. His Jack... he liked that concept. When Dave realized that he smiled just because Jack walked into a room, Dave knew he was in trouble. But this was trouble that he didn't mind at all.

Dave's face turned darker as he thought about what lay before him that night at the Club Oz. He needed to plan his approach to Venchenzo and what to say to him. This was even more important now that Jack was moving in with him. He wanted no danger to befall his possible life mate because of this situation. He wasn't overly worried about his own safety, as the Marines had taught him well in hand-to-hand combat. He was sure he could protect himself if he had to. But Jack—Jack was a different situation. Jack wasn't built for combat. Jack was built for love and lovemaking. Dave would see to it that Jack was in no danger from Venchenzo no matter what he had to do. Including giving the man what he wanted.

Dave knew Venchenzo wanted to fuck him, to collect him like some kind of trophy. He had known a couple men like that before, and neither one had gotten from Dave what they had always gotten from other men. Those types didn't give a damn about a guy beyond what they were after; they just wanted to fuck him and throw him away. If it came down to Jack's safety and there was no other way to ensure it, Dave would let the guy have his ass even though the very thought of it made him nauseous.

Dave dozed off for almost an hour, and when he woke up, he decided to take another shower and dress down for the night. This was not a night for the tight black jeans and even tighter T-shirts. This was a night for looking as unsexy as he could manage. Dave thought about dressing unsexy and laughed out loud. *How in the hell am I going to do that?*

Dave put on a pair of loose-fitting slacks and a red, long-sleeved shirt. He added loafers, but no jewelry and no cologne. When he looked in the mirror, Dave still liked what he saw, but he knew it was far from the best he could look. He was trying to project a business-like image, and he hoped Venchenzo picked up on that vibe.

When Derrick arrived a few minutes early, Dave offered him a drink.

"Actually, better not. I might need a clear head tonight, and skipping a drink is probably a good idea. I have to tell you, though; I tried to get reservations and couldn't. I was told that they were booked up the entire night for dinner. So we can just try to see him if you want."

"Well, time to test his last statement to me that I was welcome in his club any time I wanted to come. We'll see what they say at the door."

Dave finished his drink, and they headed out the door. Derrick wanted to drive to limit their exposure on the street once they left the club, so they parked in a space across from the club that was reserved for delivery trucks. Derrick knew that he wouldn't get towed or ticketed as the cops all knew his car.

As they approached the club, they noticed that people were being turned away at the door. When they got to the door, they stopped when the bouncer put up his hand.

"Sorry, guys, we're full. Try again tomorrow night."

"I'm Dave Henderson, a friend of Mr. Venchenzo's."

The bouncer checked a small black book and apparently found Dave's name. He looked up and said, "Please go in, sir, and enjoy yourself."

Dave responded by saying, "Thank you. Have a good evening."

As they entered, they saw that the club was packed, and another bouncer approached them with a hand wand. "I need to check you both for weapons," he said as he turned the wand on.

"I'm Dave Henderson, a friend of Mr. Venchenzo's."

"Sorry, sir, no exceptions." He began to scan Dave when Venchenzo came over to them. Dave guessed that the bouncer outside had called and told the boss who he had just admitted to the club.

"That's all right, Eddy. Mr. Henderson is my guest... as well as his friend there."

The bouncer backed off as Venchenzo shook Dave's hand. "I was wondering if I was going to see you in here again. You haven't been back since opening night. That's not very nice of you, Dave," he said with a smile.

"We thought we would come out and have dinner tonight. I didn't realize the club was packed. We can go. It's no problem."

"Nonsense, you came here for dinner, and dinner you'll have."

Venchenzo raised a hand and snapped his fingers, and the manager came over from the entrance to the dining room.

"Would you give these gentlemen a choice table so that they can watch the show as they eat?"

"Of course, Mr. Venchenzo. This way please," the manager gestured for Dave and Derrick to follow him.

"Oh, David, I'd like to talk to you this evening before you leave the club," Venchenzo said.

"Yes, I wanted to talk to you also. Shall we do it now?" Dave asked.

"No, no, you go eat, and then we'll talk," Venchenzo said with a smile.

Dave and Derrick were shown to a small table with a reserved sign on it. "I'll send a waiter right over to you," the manager said.

"This is probably the only time I'm ever going to be in here," Derrick said.

"Why is that?"

"If he is Mob, I can't afford to be seen in here. I *am* a cop after all."

A waiter came over and handed them both menus and took their drink order, which consisted of a Coke and a Diet 7Up. As they looked down the menu, both decided that the burger was the route to go, as it was the only dish under ten dollars, coming in at $9.95. If the burger was good, it would be worth it since entertainment came with the price of the food.

As they waited for their dinner, they looked around at the other tables and saw that most of the A-list of gay society was present in the club. Everyone was dressed up for the most part, which gave the place the feel of a club from the Roaring Twenties.

"I didn't know what we were gonna do if you had been checked at the door for a weapon," Dave said.

"Well, the only thing I could do would have been to show my police credentials."

"That would have created a fuss, I think. I'm glad Venchenzo was there to intervene."

The waiter returned with their dinner, and as they ate, a drag show began on stage. Rather than the normal type of lip-syncing, the performers were actually using their own voices and were quite good. By the time Dave and Derrick finished eating, they were beginning to have a good time and almost forgot the reason for their being there. In fact, a couple of times Dave caught Derrick's eyes looking where they shouldn't have been.

"I'm going up to see Venchenzo now," Dave said as the show ended. "His office is on the second floor of this place, and the door that leads to the stairs is to the left of the main bar in the outside room."

"Okay, if you're not back in ten minutes, I'm coming to look for you. If there's trouble, tell him that a Reading cop is sitting in the dining room with more outside waiting for a signal to hit the place. That should give him second thoughts."

"Okay, sounds good. Here goes," Dave said as he got up from the table, wiping his mouth on the napkin. He walked over and told the dining room manager that Venchenzo wanted to see him. The manager pulled out a cell phone, pressed one number, and mumbled something into the phone in Italian.

"Louie is coming to get you; please wait over there by the bar," the manager said.

As Dave leaned against the bar, he tried to mentally add up what the club was bringing in on a Saturday night, and he figured that it had to be a lot. People were drinking, eating, and having fun, and that added up to money. As he was thinking about it, Louie tapped him on the shoulder. "This way," Louie said, walking off without waiting to see if Dave followed.

They walked up the stairs and entered the second-floor bar room. There was no one in it besides Franklin Venchenzo, Louie, and Dave. Venchenzo was eating a bowl of pasta fagioli with a glass of red wine.

"Ah David, was your dinner good? What did you have?"

"Yes, dinner was good. We just had hamburgers. It was what we were in the mood for, and I must tell you they were great."

"Ah, such a shame you didn't try one of the pasta dishes. I have one of the best Italian cooks in the area working in the kitchen. Shame…. Please, sit down. Glass of wine?"

"No, thank you, and I really can't stay long. Look, we need to talk," Dave said as he took a seat in the booth next to Venchenzo.

"Oh? What do we need to talk about? Did you want to tell me you're sorry for not coming in sooner?"

"Mr. Venchenzo, you're a good man, and, I'm sure, a man of honor. You have fine things all around you, a great club, good business sense to know what will make it in this city, and I'm sure you are used to getting only the best of things. My boss at work has been making it very difficult for me because of your requests to utilize me."

"Yes, what's wrong with that? You work there as a paralegal, right? I want to deal with only the best at the firm."

"Yes, sir, but I have projects that I'm responsible for, and I have to stay on time or I could lose my job."

"Fine, you leave that place and come work for me. I'll use you right here, and you can continue to go to college, and I'll pay for it. How's that?"

"And what would you want from me in exchange for this generosity?"

"David, I'm hurt. Who said anything about you having to pay for it in some way? Can't I give you a gift?"

97

"Mr. Venchenzo, there are no free rides in this life. This I know from my time in the Marines. You want something from me. Now please tell me what it is."

Venchenzo sat back and looked at Dave. He folded his cloth napkin and put it on the table before him and looked Dave in the eyes. Dave swallowed, getting very nervous as he waited for Venchenzo to speak.

"Yes, I desire a gift from you, and for this gift I am willing to make life very nice for you. There is no limit to what you might achieve working for me. You will want for nothing, never be hungry, always taken care of by me. You want a new car? You ask and I'll get you a new car."

"And what is this 'gift' that you desire from me?"

"I want you to become my man, my lover. I want you to sleep with me. I want to enjoy the tightness of your incredible ass. For this gift, I'll give you much in return."

Dave sat back in the booth as if he was thinking about the proposition that had been put to him. He framed his answer carefully, just as he'd rehearsed it at home.

"Mr. Venchenzo, I'm truly honored that you would think so highly of me as to offer such a life to me in exchange for sex, my companionship, and loyalty. I'm moved by this proposal, but I must decline it."

"You're saying no? Why? Is there someone else in your life? Is that man downstairs your boyfriend?" Venchenzo asked angrily.

"No, there's no one in my life. As for the man downstairs, he's a friend of mine, a Reading police officer who I need to get back to shortly."

"I don't understand, David. If there's no one in your life, then why would you say no?"

"To give what you ask, I must love the man I give it to. I don't love you, Mr. Venchenzo, in fact, I hardly even know you. Therefore, I can't give you what you ask."

Venchenzo got up from the booth and paced back and forth in front of Dave. Finally he stopped and looked at Dave. "You show great disrespect for me by coming to my club with a cop. A cop! What did I do to deserve that kind of treatment?"

"Mr. Venchenzo, Derrick is a friend of mine who happens to be a cop. He did *not* come here as a cop, but as my friend."

"I get what I want in this life. If you won't work for me, you won't work in Reading, period! Do you understand me? I can make life very pleasant or very *un*pleasant for you," he warned.

Dave stood up and replied, "You might usually get what you want, but not this time. I'm not for sale, Mr. Venchenzo. Not now, not ever. Now, if you'll excuse me, I must go."

As he turned around to leave, Louie stepped from the shadows and barred the door.

"Tell him to move aside, Mr. Venchenzo. Now."

"What if I just take what I want right here and now? What then, pretty boy? What would you do then? I would get what I want, and in return, you would have nothing!"

Dave looked down at his watch and then back at Venchenzo. "If I'm not back downstairs in two minutes, my friend will send a signal to the Reading police officers waiting outside to rush this place. That would be very bad for business, wouldn't it?"

"You little son of a bitch! Get out of here! Get out and never set foot in my club again! Louie, get him out of here! That's a friend that you came with? No! It's a cop that you came with!"

Louie grabbed Dave by the arm and squeezed, pulling him toward the door. Dave reacted instinctively, going into combat mode. In three quick moves, Louie was dazed and on the floor. Dave reached over and took the .38 from Louie's waistband and threw it across the floor. Dave looked back at Venchenzo as he pushed through the door, and he went down stairs where he found Derrick waiting in the bar.

"Are you all right?" Derrick asked.

"Did you pay the bill?"

"We didn't get a bill. The guy over there said the dinner was on the owner."

"Bullshit."

Dave took out his wallet, removed a twenty and a ten dollar bill, and walked over to the manager. He stuffed both bills into the man's jacket and said, "This is for the dinner." Turning away, he left the club with Derrick.

Outside, Derrick couldn't contain his curiosity. "What happened up there? You look really bent out of shape! Are you okay? Did he do something to you?"

"The son of a bitch first tried to blackmail me by telling me I wouldn't work in this city if he put the word out, and then he threatened to rape me right then and there. That goon Louie was blocking the exit and then made the mistake of grabbing my arm and trying to pull me out the door. I put his ass on the floor! By the way, he was carrying."

"What? Are you kidding me? Do you wanna press assault charges on Louie?"

"Nah, it'd be my word against his. They'd say I was some loser trying to get at Venchenzo. Fuck him."

"I can't believe he was going to try and rape you! How'd you stop that from happening? Derrick asked as they got into his car.

"I told him you were downstairs and that you were a cop. I used the line you gave me about sending a signal to cops outside the place. That worked. Don't kid yourself though, unless Louie had pulled a gun and held it to my head, Venchenzo wasn't getting any of *this* ass!"

"Well, I'm damn glad I went with you, then. You could have ended up hurt or worse."

"Yeah, at one point, I even considered giving him what he wanted just to get him out of my hair. But when he started talking all that bullshit, I was determined that was not going to happen. Now I gotta worry about Jack's safety. He's moving in with me... maybe tomorrow."

"Got a suggestion for you. Why don't you go over to the sheriff's department on Monday and file for a concealed weapons permit. You're well trained in the use of firearms, so I'm not worried about you being a danger to the public. You can even put me down as a reference."

"Ah, I don't know about that. I kinda left guns behind, and I'm not sure I want to take up with them again. But if I see any shit going down, I might just do that. I'll talk to Jack first, though."

"Okay, just let me know. And don't hesitate to call nine-one-one if anything sketchy happens."

Dave leaned over and gave Derrick a quick kiss on the cheek when he dropped him off at the apartment. Derrick waited until Dave unlocked the door and went into the building before leaving.

Dave closed the door to his apartment, collapsed onto the sofa, and began to shake from the intense rush of the steady stream of adrenaline released into his body since he'd gone up the stairs at the club. He was trained to react to violence, but he had never enjoyed it. Putting Louie down on the floor and in mild pain was not something that Dave was happy about. He now had two enemies at the club instead of just one.

After talking with Venchenzo, Dave decided that on Monday, he was going to tell Blankenship to shove it, and he fully intended to file a labor complaint against the firm. It was inexcusable for him to have been put in that position, gay or not. The more he thought about it, the angrier he became.

Dave fixed himself a large drink and sat back down to try and mellow out. As he took the first sip, the phone rang. Dave's immediate thought was that it was the club calling to create some new chaos in his life. When he looked at the caller ID, he smiled.

"Hi, Jack, what's up?"

"I thought I saw you get out of a car and go into your building. Did you go to the club? And if so, how'd it go?" Jack asked with palpable concern in his voice.

"Yes, I made my position crystal clear regarding becoming Venchenzo's boy toy."

"Did he get mad?"

"Let's just say that I'm glad I had Derrick with me. It could have gotten real ugly, and by now I would be in some pain, I think. But I don't want you to worry about it at all, okay?"

"But you're all right?"

"Yes, I'm fine. I'm actually sitting here having a drink trying to calm down. Wanna come over?"

"I shouldn't, honey. I've got so much packing to do if I'm moving in tomorrow. You still want me, right?"

"Of that you can be sure. I feel really good about us becoming a couple, and I can't wait for you to be under the same roof as me. No trouble out of Billy?"

"He got huffy and walked toward me like he was thinking of doing something, but I put a stop to that."

"Oh, did you hit him?"

"No. I told him that he could talk to you if he didn't like the fact that not only was I moving out, but that you and I were now officially together."

Dave laughed. "Ah, I wish I could have been there to see his face. Good. As long as he's nice to you, he'll never have to be worried about me. What time can I come over tomorrow to help with things?"

"Is nine o'clock too early?"

"No, hon, that's fine. Let's get it done, and then we can have a nice dinner."

"Okay, put some coffee on tomorrow morning, will ya?"

"For you, anything."

After hanging up, Dave finished his drink with a smile and found that he was now perfectly calm. He got up, brushed his teeth, and went to bed alone for the last time. He thought about Jack as he fell asleep and realized that he had come to love this gentle sweet man and that he would more than likely become the most important person in the rest of his life. Dave couldn't help but also think about Jack's bright, straw-colored hair, and he felt his dick twitch just a little when picturing Jack naked in his mind.

Chapter 8

DAVE woke early on Sunday morning and was itching to get the move over with. The coffee pot was on, and he was out the door heading to the neighboring building by eight forty-five. He rang the doorbell twice before Jack buzzed him in.

He climbed the stairs, found the door to Jack's apartment ajar, and walked into the living room where he found boxes stacked almost to the ceiling.

Jack walked over, gave Dave a kiss on the lips, and said, "You're early."

"Yeah, guess I'm anxious to get this over with. Billy around?"

"Nope. He was up before you and went to his family's place for the day. On the way out the door, he actually said that he expected me gone by the time he got home later today."

"Damn, he's an asshole."

"He hates losing anything that he thinks is his and that includes me."

"Yeah, well, no one owns you, babe. Just remember that. Why don't I start taking these boxes over while you finish packing?"

"Okay, but don't rush it and hurt something that I might want to use later," Jack said with a snicker.

"Oh really? Baby, anything you might want to use later is in top shape and will be waitin' on you. Now get a move on, dude."

As Dave left with an armload of boxes, he saw Jack standing there for a moment smiling.

Dave was back for more boxes just as Jack was finishing up his packing. He brought the last of his things out of his bedroom and said, "That's it. Now, let's get it all gone!"

For the next two hours, they made constant trips back and forth, carrying all of Jack's worldly possessions over to his new home. They stacked everything in the living room for now so that they could get the actual move over with as soon as possible. Then they could take their time putting things away. When they came back for the last time, Jack took one last look around the apartment to make sure he didn't overlook anything, took the apartment key off his ring, and set it on the chair. There was no longer a coffee table because it had gone with Jack.

When they sat those last boxes down in "their" apartment, Dave said, "Thank God I lived next door and not a block away!"

"What? Tired? Thought you were tougher than that," Jack said with a smile.

"I'll give you tough," Dave said as he tackled Jack onto the sofa and kissed him long and deep. "Now, you're my bitch!" Dave said with a loud laugh.

"Bitch? You'll wake up bald one morning if you call me bitch again, mister!"

When they stopped laughing, they drank cups of coffee and then took the rest of the day to work on unpacking. When the last thing was put away in its proper place, both men realized they were hungry.

"I don't feel like cooking. What do you say we just go get a hamburger or a sub sandwich?" Dave asked.

"Sounds good to me. I love Italian sandwiches. Let's go to Mario's and get a couple of sandwiches with chips."

"You're the boss," Dave replied as they jumped up and headed out the door.

"I'm glad you realize that," Jack said.

"Huh? Realized what?"

"That I'm the boss," Jack said with a smile as he swatted his new lover on the ass.

As THEY were leaving the sandwich shop, Dave noticed a Cadillac Escalade going slowly down the street, but he couldn't see who was inside until the driver's window was rolled down. It was Louie. The hired muscle didn't yell anything; he just stared at Dave and Jack. Dave tried to ignore him, and he drove off.

Dave felt a combination of panic, fear, and anger at the apparent attempt to intimidate him on the street.

Jack failed to realize what was going on but must have sensed a change in his partner's mood. "What's up? You got quiet all of a sudden. Thinking about all the shit I brought with me or something?"

"Ah, no, was thinking about tomorrow at work. I'm gonna quit the firm because they're trying to make me sleep with that asshole. It's not right, and I can't continue there."

"Oh wow, you didn't tell me about that. Are you sure?"

"Honey, they tried to turn me into a whore for the bottom line. I'm quitting and filing a complaint with the Department of Labor."

"When you put it that way, I can totally understand. Can we afford for you to be out of work right now?"

"Yeah, I've got several months' worth of money for bills stashed away in that big fat bank of yours. It's all my final leave pay and regular pay that I got when I left the Marines. We'll be fine, and it won't take me that long to find another job."

"Okay, it's not like I'm exactly broke, either. I have several thousand in the bank as well."

"Several thousand? Damn, boy, you're rich! I should have asked for a dowry from you!"

"Yeah, well, it's taken me over four years to save up that much money, but if we need it, we can use it. You should have just let the man fuck you; it would have been so much cheaper," Jack teased as he ducked and ran the remaining half block to their apartment.

When he got to the front door, Dave watched as Jack realized that he didn't have keys to the building or apartment yet.

"Forget that you need keys to get in, smartass?"

"Um, yeah. Who do I see about that problem?" Jack asked with a smile.

"You gotta talk to the leaseholder of the apartment about that, and I understand that if you're cute, he makes you give him head and ass before you get your keys."

Jack laughed and replied, "Well, it depends on whether or not the leaseholder is up to my standards before I'll put out for keys."

They chuckled all the way up to the apartment and enjoyed their dinner. Both were totally exhausted from the move, and they went to bed around ten o'clock, too tired to make love.

THE next morning, Jack was up first and all done in the bathroom before Dave even opened his eyes. Dave was greeted by the aroma of freshly brewed coffee, which brought an immediate smile to his face. He jumped out of bed—morning wood and all—and walked into the kitchen nude.

"Well, is this how you greet your roommates in the morning?" Jack asked while licking his lips. "'Cause if it is, I can't understand why you didn't have a roommate or two before me."

"Only the ones that I love," Dave replied.

"Oh, you say that to all the boys; you're not bullshitting me, mister. Here, let me pour your coffee so you don't splash that rather beautiful appendage sticking out from between your legs."

"Ouch, yes, that wouldn't be too good." Dave grinned. "A man could get used to this, you know?"

"Uh huh, well, I don't mind playing Suzy Homemaker in the morning, because I know you're not a morning person. Just don't think that you've hired a housekeeper and cook, boyo."

"Never in a million years would I think that, buttercup!"

Jack spit coffee all over the floor when he heard "buttercup" again. "Now look what you made me do! You're cleaning that up!"

"Yes, dear."

Jack watched as a naked Dave got down on his hands and knees and wiped up the floor with a paper towel. Before Dave could get up, Jack walked over so that his crotch was at mouth level.

"You're asking to be very late for work. You realize that, don'tcha?" Dave warned.

"On second thought, I'll wait until you're freshly showered tonight," Jack said. "I'm off to work. Call me and let me know that you're okay after talking with the asshole at the law firm."

"Will do," Dave replied as Jack closed the apartment door.

Dave jumped in the shower and left for the office without putting on a tie. This was going to be a "no tie" day. When he got to the office, Blankenship hadn't arrived yet, so he poured himself a cup of coffee and sat down at his desk. He went through the drawers taking anything that belonged to him and when he was finished, sat back, and sipped his coffee.

As he sat there doing nothing, the officer manager came over to his desk with a frown on her face.

"Are you planning on getting any work done today, or are you just going to sit there drinking coffee?" she asked with an attitude.

"Actually, no, I don't plan on getting any work done today, if you must know. I'm waiting for old man Blankenship to get in so I can talk with him. I'll be his first appointment of the day."

"What are you talking about? What's going on?"

"That's between me and the managing partner of this zoo. You'll be informed when or if it's your business to be informed."

"I don't know what you're playing at, Dave, but that attitude is going to get you fired," she warned.

Dave stifled a yawn and took another sip of his coffee. After another forty-five minutes, the managing partner of the firm walked through the door. Before Dave could even move, the office manager was in his ear. As he got up from his desk sans coffee, Blankenship looked over at Dave and said, "I understand you want to see me?"

"Yes, that's correct. Now would be a good time."

Blankenship raised an eyebrow at Dave's response and motioned for him to follow. As they passed the office manager, she whispered to Dave. "I'm writing you up for the way you've behaved this morning."

Dave didn't even acknowledge this pronouncement. He closed the door after entering the boss's private office and sat down without being asked. When Blankenship finished putting his briefcase on the credenza near his desk, he turned around. He looked surprised to see Dave already sitting.

"Have you come in here this morning to tell me you've changed your mind about seeing Mr. Venchenzo and that you'll agree to do what's best for the firm?"

Dave chuckled. "You don't give up, do you? No, I haven't come in here to tell you anything like that. In fact, Mr. Blankenship, I've come in here this morning to tell you that I'm resigning my position with the firm, and that further, I'm filing a complaint against you and the firm for sexual harassment and for attempting to force me to prostitute myself in the financial interests of the firm. I'll also be seeking the best attorney I can find in the state to sue you and the firm for hostile work environment and anything else that lawyer can come up with to file. On that note, I'll be leaving."

Dave got up out of the chair and left the office as Blankenship was telling him to sit back down. Dave continued to his desk and finished his coffee in one gulp. "Damn, this place really had great coffee. Damn shame."

"Ah, David, I want you to talk with me about your write-up," announced the office manager.

Dave always tried to be a gentleman, as that was the way he was raised, but this woman had plucked his last nerve, so he turned on his heel and said, "I don't give a flying fuck what you want anymore, missy, because I just quit two minutes ago. So just take your little write-up and stuff it."

He threw the key to the office down on his desk and walked out without looking back. As he walked home, Dave felt a mix of emotions that ran from elation for standing up for himself to depression over having quit a job with a supposedly good law firm that was in his field. It came down to a matter of principles as to what was more important in life: a particular job or one's self-respect. He knew that he had chosen the right one.

The first thing he did when he got home was call Jack.

"Hi, hon. I quit and I'm home."

"Are you okay? Was it bad?"

"No, the office manager pissed me off, but I let Blankenship have it with both barrels. Now I need to file the complaints and hire an attorney."

"If you're gonna hire an attorney, let him file the complaint," Jack suggested.

"You're right. That's what I'll do."

"Okay, gotta run. Have a meeting in five minutes. Love you."

"Love you too. See you tonight."

Dave got some coffee and sat down with the phone book. He was going to call the local bar association and ask for a referral to a lawyer who specialized in suing other lawyers for malpractice and other offenses. Just as he found the number, the phone rang. The number of his former employer popped up on caller ID.

"Yes?"

"Dave?"

"Yes, who's this?"

"This is Mr. Blankenship. Look, I'm sorry that you perceived our asking you to interact with a client as some sort of sexual harassment, but I assure you that it was no such thing. You would be unable to prove that before the labor commission."

"Really? Well, during my meeting with Mr. Venchenzo Saturday night, which was witnessed by a police officer, I was told that he was insisting that you assign me as his personal liaison. He made it quite clear that he intended to fuck me, and in fact, I was almost raped by him. I had to defend myself from one of his hired thugs. If you think I can't prove anything, then you have nothing to worry about. Now, if you'll excuse me, I'm meeting with a reporter shortly, and I have to prepare for the interview."

Dave hung up. *Fuck 'em. Let 'em sweat.*

One minute later, the phone rang again. It was Blankenship once more.

"Dave, okay. Look, what will it take for you to be quiet and not cause any fuss for the firm?"

"I'm open to a settlement. I want a cashier's check for twenty-five thousand dollars within twenty-four hours of this phone call. If you deliver on that demand, I'll let this go, and you'll never be contacted by me again."

"You'll have to sign an affidavit to that effect. Be here at five o'clock today."

This time, Blankenship hung up, and Dave smiled. *That should take care of the rent for a while.* Dave got up and felt like a giant weight had been lifted from his shoulders. He no longer had to work for an employer who had little respect for him as a person, and he got a nice fat check to cover expenses for as long as it might take to find another job. Maybe he would go to college full time and finish sooner since he didn't have to work for a while now.

Just before five o'clock, Dave left a note for Jack that he had to run into the firm for a meeting and that he would be back shortly. It took him only seven minutes to reach the office, and he found Blankenship waiting for him with an angry look on his face.

"Close the door," Blankenship said in a brusque tone.

After Dave sat down, Blankenship slid a document across his desk. "Read it and sign it."

Dave took his time reading the document, which basically said that the firm had done nothing wrong, that there were no actionable employment practices committed against Dave, and that he agreed to remain silent about anything that had occurred during his employment at the firm. In short, if he signed the document, it was as if nothing had ever happened.

Dave recognized the document as a standard release, and he took the pen and signed. Blankenship buzzed for the office manager to come in and notarize the affidavit, which she did and quietly left. Blankenship opened his desk drawer, took out an envelope, and slid it across to Dave. Dave picked up the envelope and opened it, inspecting the check inside. It was made out to Dave in the amount of $25,000.00, as agreed.

Dave slipped the envelope into his pocket and turned to leave. But before he could get out of the door, Blankenship fired one last volley. "Don't think you'll get a job anywhere in the county, because if you try, you're in for a shock. No one will have you—no one. Now get the hell out of this office."

"With pleasure."

Dave breathed a sigh of relief as he walked back home for the second time that day. He would give the check to Jack to deposit for him in the morning. He had a little over three weeks until the end of the semester at college, and he needed to make up his mind fast as to what he was going to do.

When he got home, he found Jack already there and starting dinner. Dave walked up behind Jack, put his arms around him, and rested his head on Jack's shoulder.

"You had a meeting at the firm? How come? Did you take your job back?"

"No, but I did take away something." He pulled out the envelope and handed it to Jack. "Would you take care of that for me in the morning when you go to work?"

Jack looked at the check and whistled. "Wow, what's this for? To keep quiet?"

"You got it. It's like I never worked at the firm. We can do some talking about all this after dinner. Whatever you're making smells wonderful."

"Okay, well, may I suggest that you shower and become nice and fresh so that we can have dessert if we're in the mood?"

"Why do I have to be showered to eat dessert?" Dave asked with a puzzled look.

"I told you this morning that I wanted to get with you tonight after you were freshly showered, didn't I?"

"Ah, indeed! I'll be most happy to shower off, my dear. But first, we eat."

"And then we eat again!"

BEFORE showering, Dave jumped on the computer and did some quick checks on state universities in various states. He was looking for a possible replacement for his current college, checking the cost of attending the school. If Blankenship was telling the truth and Dave couldn't get another job here, they would have to move out of state or settle for him not working for a while.

As Dave was reading, Jack came up behind him and put his arms around Dave's chest. "Whatcha reading?"

"I'm checking out some universities. We should probably talk about this sooner than later."

"Talk about what?"

"Well, honey, if I can't get a job, which Blankenship threatened, and that asshole from the club won't leave me alone, I only have once choice left."

"To move. Is that it?"

Dave turned around in the chair so that he was looking at Jack. "Would you come with me?"

"Where to?"

"I'm not sure yet. But you're not against the concept?" Dave checked.

"No, as long as it's some place warmer than Pennsylvania weather."

"You do love me, don't you?"

"Yes, I would have to love you in order to give up my friends and family here in Reading and move away. But I think you're the man for me for the rest of my life. If that means I have to move, then I move."

Dave stood up and took Jack into his arms. They held each other for a few moments, and then Dave kissed Jack. "Thank you. I'll try to never let you down. There may be rough times once in a while, but never doubt that I love you."

Jack looked down and back up. "I can see how you love me," he said with a smile. "Now go get your shower if you want me to do anything with that."

Dave laughed, hugged Jack again, and took off down the hall for the bathroom, leaving Jack leaning over the chair and reading about the University of Central Florida.

Jack was walking down the hallway when Dave flew out of the bathroom, dripping wet with a towel in his hair and totally naked. He was still semi-erect and was working on going full mast when Jack asked, "Looking for someone?"

"Yep, you. Get your fine-looking ass into the bedroom. Now. Daddy wants to play!"

"Oh gawd! Daddy…."

Since Dave was already naked and now cast-iron hard, he pulled Jack over to the bed and began to undress him. First, he removed Jack's shirt, and when Jack stood bare chested, Dave licked each nipple, giving them a little nibble before he stopped. Next, he sat down on the bed and reach up to unbuckle Jack's belt and pull the zipper of his jeans down slowly. Jack stood there looking down at Dave, smiling, his breath quickening.

As usual, Jack's jeans were tight, just as Dave liked them, and when Dave pulled them down, down came the underwear as well. Dave pulled off each pant leg and threw the jeans on the floor and then bent down and removed the shorts that were stretched between Jack's legs. The final act in the striptease was the removal of both socks.

When Dave looked back up, Jack was fully erect as well. Dave took Jack in hand and slowly jerked his cock a couple of times, admiring the length and girth of Jack's manhood. He slowly caressed Jack's balls, which hung nicely underneath, and when he couldn't resist any more, he pulled Jack into his mouth and took him all the way to the root. Dave slowly worked his way back and forth on Jack, licking all the way. He ran his hands over Jack's bare ass, sending shivers up Jack's spine. Jack had the smoothest ass that Dave had ever encountered, and he loved running his hands over it.

Letting Jack loose, Dave swung his legs up onto the bed, scooted into the center of the mattress and faced away, then he lay on his back to look up at Jack behind him. As Dave's head hung over the edge of the bed, Jack was able to push his cock down Dave's throat and fuck his face. Dave lay there enjoying the taste and feel of Jack's cock as he watched Jack's balls swing over his eyes. He could see the beautiful curve of Jack's near perfect ass where the two mounds of flesh came together.

Jack bent slightly and played with Dave's nipples, tweaking each alternately. As the speed of his thrusts increased, he began to punish the nipples a little more by twisting on them, sending little shockwaves through Dave. Dave's cock throbbed with need as he wanted Jack's mouth and ass wrapped around his cock.

Jack leaned all the way over and—still fucking Dave's mouth—went down on Dave, sucking Dave's cock for all he was worth. Jack was able to maintain his thrusting with the bobbing of his head as he sucked Dave.

After a minute, Jack straightened up, and after a few more thrusts deep into Dave's throat, he pulled out before he blew his load. He walked away from the bed for a few seconds and then came back as Dave had adjusted himself so that his head was now on the pillows and his feet were pointed toward the footboard.

Jack smiled and crawled onto the bed, landing between Dave's thighs. As Dave looked down, Jack began to suck Dave's cock again. He ran his hands up Dave's thighs and continued onto Dave's chest where he found his nipples once more. As he tweaked them, he continued to deep-throat Dave, finally letting go of Dave's cock and going to work on his balls. He ran his tongue over both of them, taking each into his mouth one at a time, rolling them around before letting them out. Jack ran his tongue over Dave's inner thigh and downward into the crevice where Dave's ass cheeks came together. Jack brought his hands down from Dave's chest and parted Dave's ass, running his tongue into the fully accessible pack of nerve endings that made up Dave's hole. As slowly as he could, Jack ran his tongue over and over the opening, teasing the sensitive flesh, flicking his tongue like a snake. Dave reacted to this attention by practically levitating off the bed.

"Holy fuck, that feels good! Do me, baby!" Dave moaned.

Jack's response was to go even deeper with his tongue. As Dave began to thrash his head around on the pillow, Jack threw Dave's legs into the air, pushing them back toward Dave's head. This exposed the object of Jack's attention to a full onslaught of his tongue.

After a few minutes of intense attention, Dave shouted, "Stop or I'm going to come!"

Since they both wanted to avoid that, Jack pulled back and dropped Dave's legs down onto either side of his body.

"No way, too early for that, babe, way too early!" Jack said.

Dave grabbed the base of his cock and squeezed to make sure that he was able to hold back. Successful, Dave closed his eyes for a few moments and then pulled Jack up onto his chest and opened his mouth once more.

Dave knew this was a favorite position for Jack, and Dave greedily accepted Jack's cock into his mouth. Jack rocked back and forth into Dave's mouth, and at one point grabbed onto the headboard to steady himself. When it was his turn to stop a climax from building, Jack pulled out and rolled onto his side next to Dave.

Dave kissed Jack on his neck and ran his tongue down his back. He pushed Jack fully over onto his stomach and continued down, dragging his tongue ever lower. When he reached Jack's bubble-like butt, he parted the cheeks with his hands and ran his tongue down the crack from the top. When he hit Jack's entrance, he gave it a good licking, which was preparation for what was about to come. He finished by kissing each cheek and then rolling over to open the drawer of the nightstand. From there he pulled out a large bottle of lube and a condom. He shifted back down to Jack's ass, where he applied a liberal amount of lube to his finger and rubbed the outside of the entrance in a teasing manner, and when he slowly inserted one finger and had Jack groaning in response, he drove the finger in as far as he could and repeated the action. He then lubed up a second finger and inserted that one as well, making Jack begin to move around slightly on the sheets. Dave could wait no longer. He put the condom on, lubed up his cock, and rolled Jack onto his back.

"I wanna look into your eyes as I fuck you tonight," Dave said.

Jack smiled and said, "Give it to me good. I like it when you're inside of me."

Dave got between Jack's legs, pulled them up, and placed one over each of his shoulders. He lined up his cock and moved forward until he felt the head of his dick pressing against the entrance. Ever so slowly, he began to push forward, feeling the head pop through as Jack turned his head to the side and exhaled.

"Breathe. Don't stop. Just relax," Dave coached.

"I'm trying… I'm rather new at this, remember? I like it, but it hurts at first."

"I know, babe. Just relax and when you're ready, let me know, and I'll continue."

Dave fought the urge to ram it in and satisfy his lust, instead waiting for Jack to signal to go ahead. When he did, Dave moved forward, feeling his shaft begin to enter Jack, and much to Jack's credit, Dave was able to insert himself all the way without stopping again.

Dave was letting his cock rest there a moment when Jack urged, "Go ahead. Fuck me. Let me have it good!"

Dave smiled and began to thrust forward and pull back. He slowly picked up speed until he was at his preferred pace and relishing the incredible feelings of fucking someone you actually cared for and loved. Dave couldn't define why it was different; he just knew it *was* different.

Jack began to jerk himself off as Dave continued at a good pace, never slowing down. After only a couple of minutes, Dave felt his climax beginning to mount. "Are you close?" Dave asked.

"Yeah, you?"

"I can go at any time you like," Dave replied.

"Let it rip!"

Dave looked down into Jack's eyes and pounded into him with their almost simultaneous climaxes occurring. Dave arched his back as he came and let out a noise that was somewhere between a growl and a moan. Jack's breathing was rapid, and as he shot all over his chest and face, he groaned loudly as well. Spurt after spurt flowed forth from both men until they were spent. Dave dropped Jack's legs and collapsed onto Jack's chest, totally satisfied and breathless.

Both men were breathing heavily as they tried to catch their breath. Dave felt his cock begin the inevitable march backward and finally felt it slip out of his lover. He rolled over onto his back and removed the used condom, throwing it in the trashcan after wrapping a tissue around it.

Jack got out of bed, went into the bathroom, and retrieved a warm washcloth, which he used to wipe down Dave's chest and cock. As Jack went to get rid of the washcloth, Dave crawled under the covers with a feeling of total contentment and peace. When Jack got back into bed, Dave turned to look at him.

"That was incredible. I didn't hurt you, did I?"

"No, not at all, why?" Jack asked.

"Well, at the end there, I really let you have it, which is why I think I came so hard. Do you actually enjoy getting fucked now?"

"Yep. As long as you're gentle going in, I can handle the rest. Actually, there's nothing that quite feels like getting fucked. I guess, as you said before, it has to do with the prostate gland. Wild how that gland is placed there, of all places. It's like when the male body was designed, the creator put in a happy button for us!"

They both laughed, and Dave pulled Jack into his arms. They snuggled together and fell asleep with their love having deepened just a little.

Chapter 9

OVER the next few days, Dave applied at the only other two law firms that had openings for a paralegal. The interviews went well, and he didn't even mention that he had worked for Blankenship.

Neither firm hired him, and when Dave questioned the decisions, he was told he lacked the experience necessary for the position even though they had been advertised as "entry level." Dave felt slightly annoyed and depressed as he thought about the parting blast he'd received from the managing partner of his last law firm. What other field could he try for that would allow him to continue his education and still make a living? The one thing that the Marines had taught Dave was how to use a weapon well and take out the enemy, skills he wasn't sure would translate easily into today's job market.

Dave knew he didn't want to be a cop, even though he had respect for most cops and the job that they did. He needed to finish his degree and go to work for either a law firm or the district attorney. Dave was fairly confident that his reputation had now been trashed in the community hiring circles by both Blankenship and Venchenzo. The only option might be to move. It would require much more thought, and he needed to talk with Jack again.

That night, as they lay in bed, Jack soundly sleeping and Dave staring at the ceiling, Dave heard the unmistakable rattling noise of someone climbing the fire escape. The unknown intruder would stop every step or so in order to minimize the noise, but, as Dave was awake, he heard it at once.

Dave got out of bed and quickly moved to the front room where the exit window leading to the fire escape was located. He looked down from the middle window trying to see who was coming up. All that he could tell was that there was a large man on the fire escape. Dave backed into the shadows of the darkened living room to see if the man would stop at his apartment or one of the others. After another minute or so, the figure stopped at the second-floor landing and looked into Dave's apartment.

Dave slowly reached over and grabbed a poker iron from the fire place. The man outside the window began to work on the latch, attempting to flip it to the down position so he could open it and climb into the apartment.

Dave was very calm but ready for anything, and then his heart froze as he heard Jack walking down the hallway toward him.

"Go back now! Don't come any farther," Dave whispered.

Jack didn't hear him, and he continued to come toward Dave. The question was clear on his face; he was wondering what the hell Dave was doing out of bed, nude, and standing alongside of the fireplace in the middle of the night. When he got within four feet of entering the living room, Dave repeated his warning. Jack heard him this time.

"Why? What's going on?" Jack asked.

"Someone is breaking into the apartment. Now get back."

"What? Do you want me to call the police?"

"Yes, and then stay in the back. If this guy gets in, I'm going to drop him."

Jack quickly moved down the hallway and back into the bedroom where he picked up the phone and called the police. Dave heard a distinct click as the window lock was successfully turned. When the intruder looked back down at the ground to make sure no one was watching him, Dave moved swiftly across the dark room waited next to the window in a small alcove.

The window creaked open, and a man who stood over well over six feet tall entered the apartment. Dave caught site of an open switchblade in his hand, and that was all he needed to see. He brought the poker down on top of the intruder's head and laid him out flat on the floor. The knife clattered as it hit the ground and bounced. Dave turned on the lights and found none other than Louie, out cold and bleeding.

"Jack, bring me something to put on before the cops get here, please."

Five feet from the unconscious man lay the open switchblade. It was obvious that Louie was present in the apartment to do him harm.

"Who the fuck is that?" Jack asked.

"That, my dear, is the thug that hangs around Franklin Venchenzo at the Club Oz."

"You're kidding me? Oh my God, you mean that crazy bastard just tried to kill you?"

"Let's let the police determine that. Go downstairs, please, and let them in. They should be here about now."

Shortly, the police arrived and came up to the apartment with Jack. One of the responding officers was Derrick, and Dave immediately felt more secure that at least one of the cops knew what was going on.

After bending over to feel for Louie's pulse, Derrick spoke into his radio mic. "Car 15, we need paramedics at this location."

"Is he still alive?" Dave asked with concern.

"Yeah, but his pulse is real weak, and he's bleeding a lot from the crack in the head you gave him," Derrick responded. The other cops began to check out the fire escape, and a detective responded to the scene to dust for fingerprints.

When the paramedics took Louie away, they didn't know if he would live or not. It was over two hours before the police left the apartment, having taken statements and dusted for prints. Since Derrick knew the situation, formalities progressed rather quickly. The last thing Dave and Jack learned was that it looked like Louie would make it.

It was almost five in the morning when both men climbed back into bed. Dave held Jack tightly to make him feel more secure and to help him go to sleep. Dave knew Jack had to get up in three hours to get to work. Dave would make sure he did. Since he couldn't sleep, Dave lay there waiting for the sun to come up.

As Jack dragged himself out the door to go to the bank, Dave started his second cup of coffee. He called the detective assigned to his case to check on Louie's status.

"Detective Morgan? Dave Henderson here. Did the intruder from last night make it?"

"Yes, he got to the hospital in time, and it looks like he'll live… although the doctors aren't sure what shape his brain's going to be in. I also had a call an hour ago from one Franklin Venchenzo wanting the details on what happened. He was down as an emergency contact in the suspect's wallet, and the hospital called him."

"Oh great, just what I need, more trouble from him. Like I told you last night, I'm almost positive that Venchenzo sent the suspect to kill me last night. Will he try again? Do I need to buy a shotgun today?"

"Look, I can get a patrol unit to sit on your place for a couple days if you want. What you do after that is up to you."

"Yeah, it's the *after* part that concerns me, especially when Louie gets outta the hospital."

"If you see him anywhere near you, call us at once."

"How long before the trial?"

"I'll talk to the D.A. later today about this case, but I doubt it will be any sooner than four months."

"Great. I don't necessarily have to stick around here until the trial though, right?"

"No, as long as we know where you're at and can reach you with a subpoena, that's all we need."

"Okay. You'll let me know if anything happens with this?"

"You bet. You're our victim here."

"Okay, thanks for the information," Dave said, and he hung up the phone, worried more about Jack's safety than his own. For the rest of the day, Dave made plans to discuss the entire situation with Jack when he came home from work. He had to do this right, while making sure Jack was fully on board with his plan.

DAVE made dinner for them that night and after eating, Dave and Jack went into the living room. Dave was nervous, and he knew it showed on his face.

"Dave, has something happened? You look terrible."

"Well, not really, but I've been thinking all day. Look, this city is probably poisoned now for me. I think a move out of state is called for, and I don't want to drag you anywhere you really don't wanna go to. Frankly, I'm worried about the position you're in now because of last night. Once Venchenzo figures out that you're living with me and understands that you're my partner now, you become a way to get to me. I don't want you hurt or worse."

"That thought did cross my mind today," Jack said as he took Dave's hand and held it.

"I can honestly tell you that there is nothing more important to me than you. If something were to happen to you, Jack, I wouldn't be able to live with myself. It would tear out my heart."

Jack pulled Dave close, kissed him gently on the lips and hugged him. "I love you."

"I love you too," Dave responded.

They broke apart, and Jack asked, "So what's the plan, because I have no intention of leaving you or not going with you... wherever it's going to be."

Dave fought back a tear as Jack's words hit him dead on in the middle of his heart. Many men had admired him in the Marines, many men wanted to sleep with him, and some even feared him, but no man had loved him to this extent.

"I think Florida is where we should go. I've been checking out the University of Central Florida, and they have an advanced program for paralegals that is well known in the legal field. It would be good to have a degree from a university over a college. Also, there are a lot of jobs there that don't require a lot of prior experience, such as Disney World. Obviously, there are gonna be banks all over the place, so that would be good for you."

"Disney World... that's Orlando, isn't it?"

"Yep."

"You know, it's always been a dream of mine to open a small restaurant and finally put my culinary education to good use. I'm a graduate of the top chef's school in the United States, and I've been working in banking middle management. I would much rather work for myself and create a career in restaurant ownership."

"Really? That's outstanding! I had no idea, but I like that idea a lot. I hate it when people go through all the effort to earn an advanced degree or train in a particular field, and then don't get to use results of that work. We could get a loan through the Small

Business Administration to get you started. I'd do whatever I could to help you achieve this dream."

"That really excites me, actually. Not only that, but if we don't stay here in Reading too much longer, we'll have more than enough money between us to move and get settled down there. If we do this, what's the first step?" Jack asked.

"I should file an application with the university for admission. My semester here is over in about a week, so the timing is perfect in that respect. I could start all that tomorrow and fax some things to the university in Florida. They also have one of the largest veteran population of any campus in the country."

"What about the trial?"

"I'd have to stay in touch with the D.A.'s office and let them know where we're living so they can reach us for trial. That part sucks, but other than dropping the charges, there's nothing we can do about it."

"Should you think about doing that? Dropping the charges, I mean?"

"Considering that I whacked him on the head with an iron fireplace poker and put his ass in the hospital, I really should go through with the prosecution to protect myself."

"I wish we could just leave all this behind and get our lives back to normal."

"Soon, baby, I promise. You don't have any questions about a move? Or any concerns?"

"No. I trust you, and I know you'll always do the best for us. Just give me at least three weeks' notice before we need to hit the road, okay? In the meantime, I'll give it more thought."

"Sure, honey. Come here," Dave said as he looked at Jack's lips.

They sat on the sofa like a pair of teenage lovers and made out. Jack moved the action to the bedroom, and they made love again. When it was over, Jack looked pensive and turned toward Dave, saying, "I'm so glad I didn't listen to my friends."

THE next morning when Dave woke up, Jack was no longer in bed. When he looked at the clock and saw that it was a little after six, he knew something was wrong. Jack wasn't due to wake up for another hour.

Dave got out of bed and searched for his partner and found him sitting in the living room with a cup of coffee.

"Why are you up so early? Is something wrong?" Dave asked.

"Yeah. Look, I'm calling in sick today since I didn't sleep much at all last night. I slept for only about an hour after we went to bed. I've been thinking about your wanting to move away from Reading and what that means. Would you be mad at me if I said I didn't want to move after all?"

Dave sat down and asked, "What made you change your mind?"

"This is my home. Reading is where my family is and where I grew up. I have many dear friends that I've come to love. Some cheap hood moves into town and now is gonna run me and the guy I've fallen in love with out of my home? I don't think so."

"Well, he's more than just some cheap hood, dear. More than likely he's with the Mob. He also sent someone after me at our home. But I understand what you're saying. What if I can't get a job because I'm blackballed?"

"Think about where you could get a job where the influence and pressure from those clowns won't matter. Or maybe you should just go full time to college and don't worry about working for now.

We have the money that you got paid from the firm, and that will last us more than a year if we're careful. I added it all up, and it comes to just over thirty-six thousand dollars."

"Are you sure? You might be in danger because you're associated with me," Dave warned.

"Yeah, I'm pretty certain that running is not the way we should handle this thing. I mean, Venchenzo could just track us down and send men after us. The move would have accomplished nothing."

"Would you get all freaked out if I got a gun permit and a gun?"

"Well, if the Marines taught you anything, I sure hope they taught you about guns, how to use them, and all about safety. No, get a gun if it will make you feel better about us here."

"I'll call Derrick later and tell him that we're not moving and that I'm gonna take him up on his offer to be a reference for my getting a permit."

Dave got up from the chair, sat down beside Jack, and put his arms around him. "I love you so much that I don't want anything to happen to you. It would kill me."

"Well, since I would apparently already be dead, you would just be rushing to join me," Jack said with a smile.

Dave punched him in the shoulder. "Don't talk like that. I don't like it."

"Look what the hell we're talking about! Gangsters and gun permits! And you think me joking about our being together in the hereafter is over the line?" Jack asked with a laugh.

"No, but I still don't like you talking about that. Never mind." Dave sighed. "Okay, we're gonna have a busy day, then. When do you call in?"

"I have to call in at eight o'clock if I'm sick."

"Why don't we reset the alarm and back to bed and get up at eight then?"

"Okay. Thank you, honey; I feel a thousand percent better now. Are you sure you're not mad at me for changing my mind?"

"Yeah, I'm sure. It's no longer just my life. It's our lives, and you have an equal say in everything we do."

Jack was asleep five minutes after they went back to bed. Dave was wide awake and just waiting for the alarm to go off.

JACK called in sick, and Dave and Jack had more coffee as Dave made phone calls to tell people that they weren't moving after all. He was going to call Derrick and then remembered that the policeman was on midnight shift for another two nights. He would have to wait until late in the day to call him. He was able to get a hold of Detective Morgan and told him that they were no longer moving but that he was applying for a gun permit. Morgan wasn't happy to hear it.

Just after ten o'clock, Dave went to the courthouse to visit the sheriff's department and apply for the permit. He found the office on the third floor, filled out the application and paid the $25 fee.

"Okay, sit down and we'll run all the checks required. If you come back clean, we'll issue you the permit now," the deputy said.

Dave was surprised but thankful that the permit would be issued after computer checks. He had been under the impression that it would take at least a few days to get clearance. As he waited, he decided to wander over to the bulletin board, and he found a copy of open city and county jobs. Dave scanned down the list, which included positions open at the county jail for correctional officers. He paused there and thought about it. Could he go to work every day and end up in a prison? He quickly moved on and came to something that really grabbed his attention:

Internship: District Attorney's office looking for interns in both the criminal investigations and paralegal areas. Minimum wages paid for full-time college students majoring in the legal or criminal justice fields. Apply in person.

Dave recalled what Jack had said to him earlier that morning: *Get a job where their influence and pressure won't matter.* Dave hoped that the district attorney's office would be just such a place.

"Mr. Henderson?" the deputy called out.

"Yes, here," Dave said as he returned to the counter.

"You've been approved. Sign here and go over there for your picture to be taken."

After Dave finished that, he was handed a concealed weapons permit a few minutes later. Where the reason for concealment was annotated, the response was *personal protection.* Dave headed out the door and down the wide marble hallway to another door that read "District Attorney's Office."

Dave entered and was standing at the counter to be waited on when he saw Detective Morgan coming out of one of the conference rooms. The detective saw Dave and went over to him.

"Hello, Mr. Henderson. There's nothing for you to do here if you're here about Louie," the detective said. "In fact, there won't even be a trial, as you now know."

"No trial? Why won't there be a trial?" Dave asked.

"Oh, I thought you already knew. The suspect is dead. Died just after five this morning."

"What? I thought he was going to be fine? What the hell happened?"

"It seems that you didn't kill him. He acquired a fast-acting staph infection that spread to the wound in his head, which caused a stroke. He died without regaining consciousness. That's what will be listed as cause of death."

"No, I didn't know. I can't say I'm happy about it, but at least I don't have to worry about him seeking revenge."

"No indeed. If you're not here about that, why are you here?"

"Actually, I'm here to apply for an internship with this office."

"Oh, I see. That's what brought you down here today?"

"No, I came down to get a gun permit, which I now have."

"Do you own a gun?"

"No, but by this afternoon, I will."

Morgan smiled and said, "Just make sure you don't shoot yourself."

Before Dave could respond, the detective was out the door and gone.

"Can I help you, sir?"

Dave looked up at the woman who spoke. "Yes, I'm here to apply for one of the internships."

Dave got an application and some information and headed home. Even though it was only six blocks back to the apartment, he still looked over his shoulder every once in a while. It didn't pay to be lazy about security.

WHEN he got back to the apartment, Jack was waiting for him. "Are we ready to go shopping wherever you buy guns?" Jack asked.

They went to one of the few gun stores in the area, and Dave found a .380 Beretta automatic with a thirteen-round clip, which was easily concealable due to a barrel length of just under four inches. The handgun set him back about six hundred dollars, and he also bought an extra clip and two boxes of ammo. An inside the pants holster that he could wear on his right rear hip caught his eye, and he added it to the pile. The total for all his purchases came to just over seven hundred dollars, which, considering that it might save their lives, was cheap. Dave was satisfied that he had found the best weapon under the circumstances. It would be in from the warehouse in three days.

"Did you really wanna leave your banking job to open your own restaurant, or was that just wishful thinking?" Dave asked as they got back to the apartment.

"No, I'd actually like to try it. I'd like to be my own boss for a change, and I think I have what it takes to make it work," Jack replied.

The phone rang before Dave was able to continue pursuing Jack's dream.

"Hello," Dave said.

"Dave? Hi, this is Michael. We met the night of your building party that Ron hosted."

"Oh, yeah, sure. What's up?"

"Well, we wanted to invite you and Jack to a little party we're going to have this Saturday night and wondered if you both would like to come?"

"I'll talk to Jack when he gets in, and I'll get back with you. How's that?"

"That would be great. I look forward to talking to you again. Do you have my number?"

"Yeah, I have it on the caller ID."

Dave hung up, turned to Jack, and said, "We've just been invited to a party by one of the guys I met at Ron's. It's this Saturday night. Do you feel like going?"

"Sure. It'd do us good to get out of the apartment and have some fun for a change."

"Okay, I'll call him back later and let him know."

Dave spent the rest of the afternoon filling out the application for an internship and registering for school for next semester. He signed up for four classes, which made him a full-time student at the college. Now the only thing they had to worry about was Venchenzo and whether he was going to take any action against Dave for Louie's demise. Blankenship's threat had been neutralized with Dave going to school full time.

The next day, Dave took the application into the district attorney's office and filed it. He was told they would be conducting interviews during the following week and that he would be called. Jack had gone back to work, and things were slowly returning to normal.

Dave found that he was actually excited about being a full-time student, as it would mean that he would graduate sooner with his degree. If he landed the job at the district attorney's, he would have a small income in addition to the money he had in the bank. The only big decision left for them was whether Jack would become the chef he had always dreamed about being.

Chapter 10

THE weekend had arrived, and Dave was happy. He knew Jack was thrilled when he came home from work on Friday evenings. Jack loved his weekends now that he had someone to spend them with that he actually loved rather than tolerated.

Dave had made dinner for them so that Jack wouldn't have to cook after a long week at work. When Jack opened the apartment door, he yelled, "Something smells good!"

"That's just me, but thanks!" Dave replied.

"If that's you, babe, I'm gonna eat you!"

"You're gonna eat me regardless of what I smell like," Dave said with a laugh.

Jack entered the kitchen, where he found Dave at the stove finishing up the cooking. He threw his arms around Dave and hugged him from behind.

"Thanks for cooking, dear. I gotta be honest and say I wasn't looking forward to doing that tonight."

"Well, I'm always thinking of you and how I can spoil you, and this time it was by cooking. I hope you like it." Dave turned around and kissed Jack, running his hands down Jack's back and over his rear. "Hmm, that feels good," he said, referring to Jack's ass.

"If you're a good boy, maybe you can do more than just feel it later," Jack said with a smile and a twinkle in his eyes.

"Hot damn, gonna get laid tonight!" Dave sang out.

Jack laughed in response. "Oh, sit down, you horny ol' goat."

"I may be horny and I may be a goat, but I am *not* old," Dave corrected.

They chatted all through dinner, with Jack telling Dave about his day at work and how he was bored with his bank job. They talked more about Jack opening a small restaurant and what that would entail. The only real worry was Venchenzo. It seemed that this problem was still a part of their lives, and Dave didn't know what to do to get rid of the looming problem.

After dinner Jack helped Dave clean up, and then they went into the living room with coffee. Before they could really say much, the phone rang again. When Dave answered, it he found out it was Derrick on the other end.

"Hey, stud, how you doing?" Derrick asked.

"Hey, dude, not bad, and you?"

"I'm off for the next three days, so I'm doing real good. What are you doing tonight?" he asked.

"Not sure at this point, but we have no plans, why?"

"Thought maybe you and I could get together at the bar and talk for a bit and have a couple of drinks," Derrick replied.

"Well, I'm a married man now, so I don't go out unless my honey is with me," Dave answered.

Jack was listening and made a face. "If that's Derrick, go ahead and meet him. I don't have to be with you every minute of the day. Be good to get you outta my hair for a night," he said with a smile.

"Derrick, the ball and chain says I can go out with you. How's that? What time you wanna meet and where?"

"How about ten o'clock at the bar we met in that first night."

"Okay, sounds good, dude. See ya then."

"Good. You don't have to be with me every time you go out, ya know? I trust you," Jack said.

Dave leaned over and kissed his mate and smiled. "What did I ever do to deserve you?"

"You just lived right. That's all," Jack said in response.

DAVE took a shower and dressed for the bar. Since he wasn't going "fishing," he didn't need to show off his pole, so he put on underwear this time and passed inspection with Jack on the way out the door. As he exited the building, he looked around, checking for any parked cars with men inside, strangers hanging in doorways, or slow-moving vehicles. None of these things came up on Dave's radar, so he continued to the bar, which was only a couple blocks away.

He was a couple of minutes early, and it looked like he had beat Derrick to the bar. When Dave walked in, he got the usual mass stare, and then everyone went back to their drinks and conversations. After Dave made sure that Derrick wasn't there yet, he sat down on a barstool and ordered a rum and Coke.

Dave looked around and saw the usual assortment of twinkies, daddy types, and just plain guys. In other words, it was just another Friday night in Reading. A couple of minutes later, the door opened and in walked Derrick, all smiles and looking hot. He sat down next to Dave, ordered a drink, and smiled.

"So, out on bail tonight, eh?" Derrick asked with a smile.

"Yeah, Jack said he doesn't need to be with me every time I go out, so here I am. Is anything wrong or did you just wanna have a couple of drinks?"

"Well, I wanted a couple of drinks and to get laid tonight. Since you're taken now, I gotta look around for someone I haven't fucked yet."

Dave laughed at that. "If I remember right, you didn't fuck this one, but got fucked by him," he said, pointing to himself.

"Yeah, well, sometimes you feel like a nut...."

A drink arrived for Dave, bought by a guy on the other side of the bar. Dave nodded his thanks and called the bartender back over.

"Listen, Sam, no more drinks from guys. Just tell them I don't accept them, okay?"

"Sure, Dave, no problem."

"Refusing free drinks?" Derrick asked.

"Yeah, you know as well as I do that sending a guy a drink is the same thing as saying, 'Hey, I wanna fuck'. Since that's not gonna happen anymore, I don't wanna take the guy's money."

"Very noble of you, indeed," Derrick replied.

"It's only right, dude."

"Look, Dave. I wanna talk to you about your safety now that you're not moving. I'm not sure if Venchenzo's people are going to retaliate for you killing Louie, but you should expect something in the way of payback. It's not like the Mob to lose a guy and just let it go. What are you doing about protecting yourself?"

"Well, I have a concealed weapons permit now, and I bought a gun earlier today, which I pick up on Wednesday."

"What kind did you get?" Derrick asked.

"I picked up a three-eighty auto, an extra clip, and a couple of boxes of ammo. I hope I'll never need to use it."

"You ever fire one before?"

"Not really. It's a little small for me to have come across it in the Corps. But I certainly know how to use an automatic."

"Tell you what... why don't we go to the police range after you get the thing, and we'll make sure you know how to handle it and actually hit what you're shooting at?"

"Yeah, that's a good idea. Thanks, man."

"Anything else you doing?"

"Not really. Can't think of anything else that'll make things any safer. The landlord put a new locking device on that window so that it can't be popped open from the outside any longer. So the apartment is pretty safe now."

They were interrupted by a good-looking guy coming up to Derrick and asking if he could buy him a drink. The guy was young, well built, and looking for action. Derrick looked at Dave and then back to the guy. He whispered something to him and the cutey smiled and walked away.

"I got a date for later it seems. Did ya see the ass on him?"

"Yeah, very nice. So ya gonna tap that tonight?"

"Whaddaya think?" Derrick replied, and they both laughed.

As the night wore on, Derrick became more and more horny while looking at his "date" for the evening, so he said his goodbyes scooped up the cutey and left the bar. Dave finished his drink, and he, too, said his goodbyes and went on home to the man who was waiting for him.

BY THE time he hit the apartment, the alcohol was beginning to work its magic on Dave. When he closed the door to the apartment and turned around, Jack was standing there looking down at his crotch.

"I spy something that I want to taste," Jack said with a leer.

"Oh, and what might that be, my dear?" Jack didn't answer with words. He closed the distance between them, put his hand on Dave's junk, and gave a firm squeeze. Dave smiled in response and then kissed his mate. "I think we can accommodate your needs, young man."

Jack smiled again. "Did you have a good time?"

"It was all right. We talked about security and my new gun. We're going to the range next week so I can get familiar with the Berretta. Then a guy hit on Derrick, and I pretty much lost him for the rest of the night since all he could think about was the guy's ass. When they left, I left too."

"Did you see anyone there that you wanted to go home with?"

"Nothing compared to what I already have at home," Dave replied. He ran his hands down over Jack's back and over his ass, patting both cheeks.

"Shall we go to bed and fuck like little bunnies?" Jack asked.

"Well, I don't know about little bunnies, but yes, we can go to bed and rock this place."

"Let's go, then," Jack said as he took Dave's hand and walked down the hallway toward the bedroom.

"Do you want me to shower first?" Dave asked.

"Not on your life, babe. I want you *now*."

Jack lit candles as Dave stripped down to his underwear. When Jack was undressed, Dave walked up behind him, put his arms around him, and hugged him. "I love you," he said.

Dave could tell Jack was smiling by the sound of his voice when he answered: "And I love you."

Jack turned around in Dave's arms and looked into his eyes. He kissed Dave on each eyelid and whispered, "How did I get so lucky?" He kissed Dave on the neck and lips as he ran his hands down Dave's front, stopping to cup Dave's balls through his underwear. He ran his hand over the ridge that had been formed by Dave's erection and jacked him slowly as he kissed him once more. Then Jack shoved down the shorts, went down on his knees, and removed them for Dave.

When he looked at Dave's cock, Jack flicked his tongue, catching a drop of pre-come that had formed on the head. As Dave moaned, Jack ran his tongue down the underside of the shaft and down onto his balls. He licked Dave's balls and took them into his mouth one at a time, sucking ever so gently, releasing each one fully bathed. Dave's knees began to go weak, and Jack rose and pushed him down onto the bed. He then removed his clothes and returned to his knees where he went back to work on Dave's cock once more. He worked his tongue over both sides of the shaft and then swallowed Dave's entire cock down as far as he could go. Then Jack let Dave's cock free and instead shoved his tongue down into the crevice that divided Dave's ass and teased the opening without really touching it.

Jack moved back up to Dave's balls and cock and then continued up Dave's body, stopping at the nipples. He went from one to the other, licking, nibbling, and sucking each until they were as rigid as Dave's dick.

Dave finally grabbed Jack and pulled him up to his lips, sinking his tongue deep into Jack's mouth. He rolled Jack over and continued to kiss him, only releasing Jack's lips to take possession of his nipples. From there, Dave began to kiss Jack everywhere that he could, working his way down Jack's thin, firm body. When he got to Jack's manhood, he kissed, licked, and sucked the head before working the rest of the shaft over with his tongue, darting down quickly onto Jack's balls.

"Fuck, that feels good, honey," Jack said. "Can I face fuck you?"

141

"Sure, babe, how do you want me?"

"Get on your back and hang your head over the edge. That's my favorite position."

"Actually, it's mine too."

Dave swung his body around on the bed and positioned himself over the edge as he watched Jack rubbing his cock. When he was set, Jack moved forward aiming his erection at Dave's mouth, entering all the way in until his balls were resting against Dave's forehead. Jack pulled back slowly, and Dave took in air through his nose as Jack began to slowly fuck his face. Dave had his head tipped back far enough that it was a straight shot into his mouth and down his throat.

Dave watched Jack slide in and out, feeling the heavy balls hit his forehead each time Jack went deep, and admired the motion of Jack's beautiful ass as it moved backward and forward. Dave reached down and began to jerk off. Now Jack could watch Dave playing with himself as well as his cock sliding in and out of Dave's mouth.

Jack bent over and took Dave's hard-on into his mouth, sucking in about four inches of meat as he continued to pump into Dave's mouth. As he sucked Dave's cock, he reached out and played with Dave's nipples, tweaking them occasionally. He must have been about to come, because Jack released Dave's cock and stood back up, slowing his thrusts to almost nothing.

Dave began to jerk off once again. He felt an orgasm building, and this was how he wanted to get off tonight. He signaled to Jack that he was near the end by pulling on Jack's ass. Jack began to fuck Dave's face once more, and Dave picked up the pace of jerking off. Jack sped up to full force with no sign of planning to stop his orgasm.

When Jack shot the first volley of come down Dave's throat, Dave began to come at once. As Dave moaned with a mouth full of dick, he shot stream after stream up onto his chest and face as Jack continued to spurt.

Finally, both men were spent, and Jack pulled his long, still-fat cock out of Dave's mouth to let him breathe easily. Both men fought to regain control over their breathing. Jack fell back onto the bed and lay there for a couple minutes. As his heart rate calmed down, Dave reached under the edge of the bed and found the towel that had he'd placed there for clean-ups. Still breathing fairly hard, he used it on himself, rolled slightly so that he could wipe off Jack's cock and balls, and then threw the towel into a clothesbasket that was next to the wall.

"Fuck, that was some good sex," Dave said.

"Yeah, it kinda curled my toes, that's for sure," Jack replied.

Jack fully recovered first and offered to get sodas for them. As Dave waited for Jack to return, he shifted around on the bed into a normal position. By the time that Jack set the drink down on the end table, Dave had recovered.

"That was really good," Dave said in a kind of dreamy state.

"Sex with you is always good, hon, and I've actually learned a few things from you."

"Well, that's only natural since you weren't that experienced to begin with. But I'm happy to teach you everything I know twice," Dave said with a big smile.

"See, that's what I love about you! You're so generous!" Jack said as they laughed.

"Come on, hon. Snuggle down into the covers with me," Dave suggested.

Jack took a long gulp of his drink and slid down next to Dave. Jack felt so warm in Dave's arms that Dave never wanted Jack to leave them. Dave was afraid one day he would wake up and discover that Jack was just a dream.

THE next evening, they got ready for the party. Jack dressed in his painted-on jeans and a light yellow polo shirt and sneakers. He put on a small gold chain around his neck and wore a simple ring on his left hand.

Dave dressed casually as well, but wore black 501 jeans that showed off his bulge just right coupled with a white Adidas T-shirt with a breast pocket. He wore black socks with black loafers. They checked themselves out in the mirror and saw that together, they made a truly stunning couple. They were sure to turn heads at the party.

They had a quick drink before leaving. Over the rim of his glass, Dave looked his partner up and down and licked his lips. "Jack, you look so good tonight, I can't stand it."

Jack leaned into Dave, gave him a kiss, and then tweaked his nipples real fast.

"Hey! Don't start something you're not going to be able to finish right now," Dave warned.

"Should we drive or walk?"

"It's a little farther than we're used to walking, so why don't we just take the car?" Dave said, secretly worried about being out in the open for that long.

"Sure, no problem. We'll get home quicker that way too," Jack added with a smile.

"You are one very horny guy, you know that?"

"Well, with you around all the time, I can't help but be horny," answered Jack.

"You're so sweet. That's why I love you."

As PREDICTED, when Dave and Jack walked into Michael's, all the heads turned and checked out both new arrivals. Dave loved the attention, if he were honest, but he knew Jack was a little more shy.

Michael came over and hugged both of them. "Glad you guys got here! Most everyone else I invited is here, so relax, mingle, and I'll get you drinks. What would you like?"

"Scotch on the rocks?" Jack replied.

"You got it, and you, Dave?"

"I'll have a rum and Coke, if you have it."

"We do indeed." Michael turned around to the living room full of people and waved his hand to get everyone's attention.

"Everyone, this is Dave and Jack, for those of you who don't already know them. I'll leave it up to you to introduce yourselves," Michael said. And he headed for the bar to make their drinks.

As everyone introduced themselves to Jack and Dave, someone put some music on, and the host announced that the buffet line was ready. Everyone made a mad dash for the food as if they hadn't been fed in a week. Jack actually laughed out loud and was pulled along by the other guys. Dave was stuck in the back of the line as he hadn't moved quickly enough.

After several minutes, Dave had his red plastic plate full of food and was headed back into the living room to find Jack so that they could eat together. When he made his way to the entrance of the room, he saw Jack standing with his back to him talking to another guy. As Dave was able to move forward, he saw the guy with Jack slip his hand around to rest on Jack's ass and then give it a squeeze.

Jack moved his hips in an effort to get the guy's hand off him without spilling the food and drink he was holding. Dave increased his speed to get to Jack when he saw the guy put his hand back on

Jack's ass. Dave got within a couple of feet and could just hear the conversation.

"Look, I'm here with my lover so I'm not interested in anything, okay?"

"Let me show you what a real man is like… you won't regret it," the other man said.

Dave put his food and drink down on a nearby end table and pulled the guy's hand off Jack, twisting it slightly.

"I guess you didn't hear my lover say that he wasn't interested. As for finding out what a real man is like, he's done that already. Now fuck off, asshole!" Dave said menacingly.

"Yo, there's no reason to get nasty here, dude, just because I was talking to Jack."

"You were doing more than just talking to Jack; you had your paws on his ass. Now do we need to go outside and have me kick the living shit out of you?"

"Oh, you're a real badass, huh? You think you're man enough to do that?"

As Dave moved in to take the guy by the throat and take him outside, Michael stepped in between them and told "Donald" to chill out or leave. He then turned to Dave and said, "Please, Dave, can you let it go this time?"

"Sure, Michael, but this asshole's been warned."

"Honey, calm down, please. It's all right. I was handling it," said Jack.

"Handling it, huh? His hand was all over your ass. That didn't look like handling it to me."

"Wow, rather caveman like, no?"

"Caveman, my ass. I'm just protecting what's mine," replied Dave.

"'What's mine'? Am I a piece of property? Am I luggage?"

"Yes, but you're Louis Vuitton!" Dave said with a smile.

"Didn't know you were so possessive. We'll talk later," Jack said.

The guys sitting on the sofa who were watching the drama unfold parted to allow Jack and Dave to sit down and eat. Dave and Donald sat across the room from each other, launching daggers for the rest of the night.

"Let's go, okay?" Dave asked about an hour later.

"Are you sure?"

"Yeah, that ass clown ruined my night."

"Okay, let's go, then."

They got up and found Michael in the kitchen.

"We're gonna head on out, Michael. Thanks for the invite. Sorry about the thing earlier," Dave said.

"Damn, I was hoping you guys weren't gonna bail out early tonight. I'm sorry that Donald doesn't quite know how to behave himself. Please don't hold it against me."

"We wouldn't do that, Michael. Thank you very much for the invitation. We'll have a party soon, and you're on the list," Jack replied.

They said goodbye to some of the guys on the way out, and Dave shot Donald a "fuck you" look as he passed by. Much to Donald's credit, he did not respond. As they got in the car, Dave began to release the tension in his body that had prepared him to fight should it be necessary. Jack mumbled about the incident all the way to the apartment. Dave got called a caveman once or twice more before they reached their happy home and got upstairs.

"Did you ever think that you might have been the one to get handed his ass in a fight? Donald is a pretty big guy, and what happened certainly wasn't worth you getting hurt in a stupid fight."

"You've got to be shitting me! You think that bag of worms could kick my ass? He would have been one hurting motherfucker by sunrise, I guarantee you that!" Dave said getting himself all angry once more.

"Okay, but please, keep your cool if something like that happens again. I'm not the type of guy who likes my man fighting in the street because someone besmirched my honor. Having you in one piece means a whole lot more to me."

"I'll try. But that scumbag knew we were together. He fucking saw us come in together!"

"Okay, okay, let it go, honey, please?" Jack said as he looked up at Dave.

"All right."

Dave went down the hallway and into the living room where he flicked the television on and tried to find a movie that fit his mood. He landed on "A Nightmare on Elm Street," and Dave smiled.

When Wednesday rolled around, Derrick came over and picked Dave up, and they went to get Dave's gun from the store. While Dave was signing all the paperwork, Derrick checked the gun out for any obvious defects and found none. Dave put the holster into his waistband, loaded the weapon, and holstered it. Dave had to admit that he felt a little more secure now that he was armed.

"Look, I can't go shooting today, but I'll let you know about next week, okay?" Derrick asked.

"Sure, that's soon enough. I really appreciate your coming by today. By the way, how did your date go Friday night?"

"Ah, baby, that was one fine man. When I got his clothes off, I practically mauled him. He was a total bottom, and I took my time once I was in him. I pounded that thing for like a half hour. Shit, if you were still single, I would for sure set you up with him. He sucked my dick like a Hoover too."

When Dave stopped laughing, he replied, "Sounds hot. You gonna see him again?"

"Hell yeah, I'm gonna see him again. When you find a natural sex machine like him, you don't tap it once and go."

"Good, maybe he'll take you off the market."

"Ya never can tell. That's how fine he is."

When Dave got back to the apartment later and closed the door, the phone began to ring.

"Hello?"

"Mr. Henderson?"

"Yes?"

"This is Paula at the district attorney's office. We'd like to see you tomorrow at one o'clock for an interview for the internship position. Can you make it?"

"Yes, I can be there at one."

"Excellent, see you tomorrow, then."

Dave hung up the phone and smiled. The day was turning into a *very* good day. Maybe things were going to work out just fine.

A WEEK later, Dave and Jack celebrated the fact that Dave was chosen for the internship and would start working at the district attorney's office the following Monday. Even though it paid only minimum wage, the experience for his job résumé would be invaluable.

Dave had cooked dinner in celebration of the good news, and they had just sat down when the phone rang.

"Why does that damn thing always seem to ring at dinner time?" Dave wondered aloud.

"Hello?"

"Mr. Henderson?"

"Yes?"

"This is Andy Milton at police dispatch. Officer Derrick Whitechek is asking to meet you at 5th and Bridge Road in ten minutes. Can you meet him?"

"Did he say what it was about?"

"No, sir, I'm afraid not. He just said it was urgent. Shall I tell him that you'll be in route to that location?"

"Yes, all right. I'm leaving now."

"Very good, sir, I'll pass that on."

When Dave came back into the kitchen, Jack saw that something was wrong.

"Derrick is asking me to meet him at 5th and Bridge... says it's urgent. I'd better go," Dave said.

"Can't you eat first?" Jack asked.

"No, he wants to meet in ten minutes. Would you put my dinner in the microwave, and I'll heat it up when I get back?" Dave bent down, kissed Jack, and went into the bedroom where he put on his gun and grabbed his wallet.

On the way out, Jack stopped him. "Do you want to take the car?"

"Nah, I don't know what he wants or where we might go. Best to just hoof it on over there."

"Be careful," Jack said as Dave went down the hallway and out of the apartment.

As he walked quickly down the street, Dave ran various reasons for the sudden summons through his mind. What could Derrick possibly want?

Chapter 11

WHEN Dave arrived at the corner of 5th and Bridge, he expected Derrick to be there waiting for him. He was surprised when he didn't see Derrick, and he moved back into the entrance to a small grocery store to be less conspicuous.

After he'd waited for an additional thirty minutes, he decided to call into police dispatch to find out why Derrick was delayed. He found a booth that still had its phone connected and dialed 911.

"Nine one one, what's your emergency?"

"Hi, you guys called me to tell me to meet an officer at 5th and Bridge. He's not here, and I'm calling to find out why not," Dave explained.

"Give me your name and who you were supposed to meet."

"My name is Dave Henderson, and I was supposed to meet Officer Derrick Whitechek over thirty minutes ago."

"Hold on, sir, let me check," the operator said as she placed Dave on hold.

A minute later the emergency operator came back on line. "Sir, we have no record of anyone here calling you and asking you to meet Officer Whitechek."

"What? I received a call at my home from you guys telling me to get here. I think the guy's name that called was Milton."

"Sir, we have no one by that name who works in dispatch. I'm sorry, sir, it appears someone played a prank on you."

"Yeah, some joke. Thank you," Dave said as he slammed the phone down. *Son of a bitch!*

Dave began the walk back to his apartment in an angry mood trying to think of who would have pulled this stunt. Poor Jack, left all alone to eat dinner while with him running around like a fool out here.

When Dave put the key in the apartment door, it opened inward. The door was unlocked, and Dave entered the apartment in a very worried state. Given the circumstances, Jack would never leave the door unlocked.

"Honey, I told you to keep the apartment door locked. Why was it open?" Dave shouted.

There was no answer. "Honey?" Dave shouted again as he went down the hallway. Again, there was no response. Dave began to get a very bad feeling. Pulling out his gun, he pushed the safety off. He entered the kitchen slowly, listening for the slightest sound.

Dave looked at the table and saw that one of the two kitchen chairs was overturned and food remained on both plates. Jack had never had a chance put his dinner into the microwave. Panicked, Dave ran to the bathroom and then to the bedroom, finding both empty. He checked the change jar where both coins and folded money were kept. It was all still there. He then ran back down the hallway to the living room and checked the latch on the window. He found it was still secure.

As Dave stood there trying to figure out what had happened and where Jack had gone, the phone rang. Dave smiled, thinking it was Jack calling to tell him he had to run over to his family due to some domestic emergency. He was going to yell at Jack for not leaving a note. He yanked up the phone and said, "Okay, where are you?"

"Mr. Henderson, Mr. Venchenzo would like to see you. He would like to see you now. Come to the club and use the back entrance."

"I don't want to see Venchenzo, and I thought he would have gotten the message by now!" Dave yelled into the phone.

"If you want to see Jack again in one piece rather than spread around on the floor, you'll get here at once. If you call the police, Jack will never be seen again. Any questions?"

"If you motherfuckers hurt him even slightly—" The phone went dead.

They had Jack, his Jack, the new love of his life, and they were threatening to harm him if he didn't do what they said. Dave wondered what he should do. Should he call the police anyway? What proof did he have? Should he just walk into a trap?

Dave concluded that he had no choice but to do as he was told. He quickly sat down and took out a pen and paper. He wrote down everything that had just happened, folded the paper, and put it in an envelope. He wrote Derrick's name on the outside of the envelope and left the apartment. He knocked on the door Ron's apartment.

"Hey, Dave, what's up? You look like you've seen a ghost," Ron said.

"Look, I don't have time to explain. If I don't knock on your door by midnight, phone the police and give them this envelope. Do you understand? If you don't hear from me, do this! Promise!"

"Okay, I promise, but I don't understand what's going on!" Ron said as Dave ran down the staircase and out the front door of the building.

"WHAT the hell is going on now?" Ron said aloud to no one who could hear him. He went back into this apartment and stared at the envelope. He saw Derrick's name on it and began to panic. Going to his phone, he dialed Derrick's cell phone number.

"Hey, Ron, what's going on?" Derrick said when he answered the phone.

"Hi, Derrick. Look, I think there's something seriously wrong going on. Dave just handed me an envelope with your name on it with instructions to call the police and give this to them if I don't hear from him by midnight tonight. Then he just ran out of the building."

"Shit. That's all you got? No idea where he was going or what was wrong?"

"Nope, that's all I got, but I don't like it one bit," Ron exclaimed.

"I agree. I'll be right over to get that envelope."

The phone went dead, and Ron sat down, feeling like he had done the right thing. He watched out the front window, waiting for Derrick to pull up so that he could go down and meet him with the envelope.

DAVE put his hand on the back door handle and it turned. He pulled the door open and walked into the Club Oz with much trepidation. As he walked forward, one of Venchenzo's men came out of the shadows and stopped him.

"Lean against the wall," the guy said.

Dave complied, and the gun was discovered and taken from him. He was then escorted up the staircase to where Venchenzo was waiting. A look of evil spread across the club owner's face when he saw Dave come into the room.

"Well, I knew you'd be back here somehow. You've been a bad boy, David, a very bad boy."

155

"Where's Jack and what have you done to him?" Dave demanded to know.

"Tsk, tsk, now that's bad manners to ask something in that tone. You need to be punished."

"How do I know you even have Jack?"

"Jerome, turn on the set," Venchenzo ordered.

From across the room, Dave saw Jack's face flicker onto the large television screen. Dave saw that Jack was sitting in a chair with a man standing next to him holding a gun to Jack's head. Dave attempted to lurch forward but was grabbed by the man who'd brought him upstairs.

"I'm going to punish you, David, for all of the trouble you've caused me. You also caused the death of a dear associate of mine, for which you have to pay."

"You sent that goon to harm me and I defended myself. If anyone's responsible for his death, it's you for sending him in the first place!"

Dave felt a crack to the back of his head and the room went dark.

WHEN he came to, he was naked and tied face down to a long bench with his legs spread. His head was aching, and when he attempted to lift it, pain shot through his head and eyes. When he was finally able to focus, he saw Venchenzo standing in front of him.

"Here's how it's going to work, David. You're going to be whipped for the trouble you've caused me. The whipping will continue until you say you were wrong and ask for my forgiveness. Then maybe I'll consider stopping your punishment. Now, to get Jack back will take a little more."

"Jack has nothing to do with this! Let him go!"

Venchenzo nodded, and Dave heard a loud crack and then felt a harsh sting on his ass from the strap that had lashed his flesh. He flinched but didn't react verbally to the pain.

"As I was saying, for you to get Jack back, you're going to have to ask me... no, you're going to have to plead with me to fuck you. If I'm convinced of your sincerity, I will fuck your tight little ass once or twice. If I'm not pleased with your cooperation in making my fuck a good one for me, I'll have my men fuck you also. By the time the sun rises, David, you're going to be a wide receiver!"

The men in the room broke out in laughter. Venchenzo nodded again, and the beating began. Tied tightly, Dave couldn't move in any way to protect himself and took blow after blow from the wide leather strap that dug into his flesh with each stroke.

Venchenzo was seated in a chair off to the side eating an apple as Dave took the beating. He occasionally smiled at a particular sound that indicated that the blow had struck solidly. Dave was withering under the intense punishment and began to pray that it would end soon.

RON opened the door and handed the envelope to Derrick, who ripped it open and read it while standing there. When he got to the bottom, he said, "Fuck!"

Derrick flipped opened his cell phone and dialed dispatch. When he got the operator on the phone, he explained that he needed backup at the Club Oz and then jumped back into his car and sped away without telling Ron what was going on.

When Derrick got to the club, the first patrol car had just arrived, and when one more unit joined them, he quickly explained to the men what he believed was happening inside. Together they tried to enter the club but found the doors locked. Derrick pounded on the door repeatedly but got no response. They went to the rear of the club and found that door locked also. Pounding on it got the same answer they had gotten at the front. Nothing.

DAVE'S ass was a bright red now, and Venchenzo signaled for the punishment to cease. Dave was near tears from the intense pain, but he was determined not to let Venchenzo see him cry.

"Wow, David, you should see your beautiful ass. It's a nice deep red with lots of marks and welts all over it. Should I let it continue or do you have something to say to me?"

Dave tried to think what he should do, but the pain was a big distraction. He knew he couldn't take much more of the abuse he was receiving. "Mr. Venchenzo, please, I *am* sorry for any trouble I may have caused you. Please, I ask for your forgiveness and that you please let Jack go."

"Hmm, Dave, I'm not sure I believe you or not. You don't sound very convincing. I think you need more," he said as he nodded to the man with the strap. The beating began again. With each stroke of the strap, Dave's resistance to complete submission grew less and less. He tried to think of Jack's face and how much he loved him. He tried to think about the happiness that was yet to come if he could just get out of this situation.

The beating stopped again. Dave repeated his apology with more emphasis this time as a phone rang in the background.

"Well, I think I believe you this time, David. Your punishment is over. Now, is there anything else you want to ask me?"

"Yes," Dave managed to choke out. "Will you fuck me, Mr. Venchenzo?"

Before Venchenzo could respond to the request, he was interrupted by one of the men. "Mr. Venchenzo, it's the police. They say there are cops downstairs that want to get in and that if we don't open the door, they'll break it down. What do you want us to do?"

Venchenzo turned on Dave and yelled, "You called the cops after I warned you not to do so. I told you what would happen if you called them!"

"I didn't call the cops! I swear!" Dave responded.

"Then who did?" Venchenzo yelled at Dave again.

"I don't know, but it wasn't me!"

"Untie him, dress him, and take him down to the basement and hide him," Venchenzo ordered. Dave had trouble standing, let alone walking because of the brutal treatment he had received, as they took him down the back stairs to the basement in just his underwear.

WHEN the door opened, Derrick and the other cops burst through, yelling for everyone to keep their hands where they could be seen.

"Where is David Henderson?" Derrick asked Venchenzo.

"I haven't seen David in a couple of weeks now, officer. Why do you look for him here?" Venchenzo responded.

"We have information that you're holding David Henderson and Jack Stonner here against their will! Where are they?" Derrick demanded to know.

"I told you, officer, I haven't see David in weeks, and I don't even know who this Jack person is."

"Then you won't mind if we search?"

"Not at all. Just show me your search warrant," he replied.

"We don't have a warrant, but I can get one!"

"Then I suggest that you do exactly that. When you come back with a properly executed warrant to search the premises, I will permit it. Until then, you'll have to leave."

"If you make us get a warrant, we'll put men on your front and back doors until it arrives. No one will come in or leave the premises. Is that what you want? In all likelihood, you won't be opening on time tonight."

Venchenzo frowned. "Get your warrant," he said, and he turned on his heel, leaving the entrance as his men stood there blocking the way of the cops.

DAVE'S heart sank. He was dragged back upstairs from the basement and once again stood in front of Venchenzo, who was clearly fuming over this unexpected intrusion into his plans for revenge. Dave had been certain that he had been saved from this ultimate humiliation at the hands of this cheap gangster.

Venchenzo stared into Dave's eyes and said, "You were in the process of asking me something?"

"I was asking you to fuck me," Dave responded quietly.

"You *want* me to fuck you, is that correct, David?"

"Yes, Mr. Venchenzo, I want you to fuck me. Please promise you'll let Jack go unharmed."

"Yes, I can promise you that. Take your clothes back off, now!"

Dave looked down at the floor, trying to control another painful spasm that was racking his ass. When he began to comply, Venchenzo ordered his men out of the room. He walked over to his desk, swiped everything on top of it onto the floor, opened a drawer, and pulled out a tube of lube.

When Dave was fully naked again, Venchenzo looked him over with a clear show of lust in his eyes. "Get over here," he ordered.

Dave meekly walked over to the desk and said, "Yes, sir."

"There, that's being a good boy. I think that ass whipping did you a lot of good. Now, lean over my desk here and spread your ass cheeks. I'm gonna give you a fucking that you'll never forget. It would have been a lot nicer for you if you had just given me what I wanted a couple of weeks ago. I might have actually cared if you were enjoying my cock. Now, not so much," he said with a leer. "Remember, if you're good and I really enjoying dumping my load in your ass, then you won't have to take on my men as well, so make it good. Now bend over!"

Dave turned around and bent over the desk. He reached back and spread his cheeks for Venchenzo to enter him without needing to guide his cock. Venchenzo looked down and smiled as he lubed up his very large cock. "I'm going to enjoy this fuck so much! Did I tell you it takes me a long time to come?"

As soon as Dave felt the tip of Venchenzo's cock touch his hole, he swung around, grabbed Venchenzo by the back of the head, and slammed the gangster's face into the desk a few times, quickly putting his hand over Venchenzo's mouth to stifle the shout of pain. He pulled Venchenzo's head back, looked deep into the gangster's frightened eyes, and smiled as he shot his right knee hard into Venchenzo's back.

Dave grabbed Venchenzo's underwear from the foot of the desk and shoved the soft cotton into the would-be rapist's mouth, making a gag out of it. Fury had taken over Dave. He was fighting to get it under control so that he didn't blow Jack's rescue. While leaning against Venchenzo to keep him in place, Dave yanked the phone cord free and used it to tie the mobster's hands behind his back.

When Venchenzo was secured, Dave grabbed his clothes and got dressed. He walked over to the counter where the man who had searched him had stashed his gun and cell phone. Dave returned to where Venchenzo was bleeding on the floor and tried to figure out his next move.

He could go down the back stairs and out the door, but that wouldn't help Jack at all. He got down on the floor next to Venchenzo, jammed the gun into the gangster's balls, and said, "Listen to me, asswipe. I'm going to blow your fucking nuts off right here and now if you don't tell me where you're holding Jack. If you think I'm bluffing, just refuse to tell me," Dave warned. "I'm kinda hoping you'll say no."

He took the shorts out of Venchenzo's mouth so the dirtbag could answer. "I swear I'm gonna kill you and chop your lover up into little pieces, you son of a bitch!"

Dave shoved the shorts back into Venchenzo's mouth and then punched him in the balls as hard as he could. Venchenzo turned red, and then blue as he rolled from side to side in agony.

"Look, you little fuck, I'm not joking. I will de-nut you here and now if you don't do as I say! Are you going to do it?"

When Venchenzo didn't respond, Dave shoved the gun back up in between Venchenzo's nuts and pulled the hammer back on the .380. Venchenzo then tried to yell in a muffled tone indicating that he would do as Dave demanded.

"You're one lucky fuck. You were just about to lose your jewels, you bastard!" Dave pulled the shorts back out of Venchenzo's mouth and once more demanded to know where Jack was being kept.

Venchenzo didn't play around this time and answered. "He's at one of my houses, the one on North 13th Street."

"Has he been hurt in any way?"

"No, no, I swear! He's just fine!"

"You better be fucking right! Here's what you're gonna do. You call there and tell them to take Jack back to the apartment immediately. You understand?"

"Yeah, I understand."

"One wrong word or sign, and I'll kill you *after* I take your nuts. You got it?"

Venchenzo nodded his head. Dave opened the cell phone, and Venchenzo gave him the number. When the phone on the other end began to ring, Dave handed the cell over to Venchenzo.

"Hey, Venchenzo here. Take the kid back to his apartment unharmed and leave him there. You got that? Do it quickly."

Dave took the phone back from Venchenzo's ear and mouth and turned it off. "Good boy. Now, if everything goes well, I'll be outta here, and you'll be free. I'm gonna warn you though, if you ever fuck with me or Jack again, I'll hunt you down and kill you. The Marines taught me the job of killing very well, and I won't fail no matter how many goons you have around you. In fact, maybe it'd be a good idea if you left Reading. There are plenty of other towns in this state for you to operate out of. Just leave us *and* the city alone."

While Dave was waiting for enough time to have passed for Jack to get home so that he could call and confirm it, one of the goons knocked on the door.

"Tell him to go away!"

"What about 'don't disturb me' did you idiots not understand? Get lost!" Venchenzo yelled.

"Okay, boss, just checking to make sure everything's fine," the goon responded.

"David, we could have had it so good, you and me," Venchenzo said. "Why didn't you go for it?"

163

"I'm particular about who I fuck, and you're not my type. If I knew that was the price tag of that bottle of champagne opening night, I would have sent it flying back atcha. You and me? Never gonna happen."

"You could have had anything you wanted, and you threw it away. For what? Some dumb little blond?"

Dave got down in Venchenzo's face and said, "The one thing I want is love, and baby, like the saying goes: you can't buy love. I'll take my little ordinary blond guy over the likes of your kind any fucking day of the week. You haven't a clue as to the meaning of life. You're a parasite that feeds off society, contributing nothing to the general well-being of the world. When you leave this life, it will be like you were never born. That's the net affect you'll have had on the world."

He dialed his home number and was hugely relieved when a very frightened Jack answered the phone. "Are you all right, honey?" Dave asked.

"Yeah, they just dumped me at the apartment a minute ago. Where are you?"

"I'm kneeling over Venchenzo in his office. Did they hurt you in any way?"

"No, I'm fine. But, Dave, I'm worried about you. You need to get the fuck out of there, now!" Jack said.

"I'm good. I'm gonna call Derrick in a second and tell him to expect me at the back door. Everything is gonna be all right, honey. Just try and relax. Maybe we'll take a vacation and get away from the city for a while. I'll see you shortly. I love you."

Dave hung up and looked at Venchenzo again. "Here's the deal. You agree to leave town, take all your goons with you, and never have any contact with me or my loved ones again; and I'll tell the cops that there was a misunderstanding, that I came here of my own free will, and that there are no problems. I have seven years to file charges against you, because the crimes that you and your little band of merry goons committed tonight are felonies. Or, I tell the truth as soon as I'm with the police. Which is it to be?"

"I agree. I'll close the club and leave. None of this had to happen if you had just given me what I wanted."

"Smart man. If I ever see you anywhere near me or Jack again, I'll kill you without a second thought."

Dave got up and walked to the door that led down the back stairs. He flipped open his cell phone and called Derrick. The policeman answered at once.

"Derrick, I'm coming out of the back door of Club Oz. Can you meet me there?"

"Dave, thank God! I'll be around there in one minute. Get outta there if you can."

Dave looked back at Venchenzo, who was crawling out from behind his desk with dried blood all over his face. "Untie me, David. I don't want my men to see me like this."

Dave shook his head, opened the door slowly, and went down the staircase and out the back door into the arms of Derrick and the Reading police.

Chapter 12

"DAVE, what the hell was going on? Luckily, Ron called me and gave me the letter you gave to him. Are you ready to press charges?" Derrick asked.

"Can I see you somewhere private for a minute?"

"Sure, come with me," the cop replied as they headed for a police car.

When they were alone inside, Dave began to explain. "They kidnapped Jack and were holding him at another location to blackmail me into coming to the club this evening. I was taken upstairs, and Venchenzo ordered one of his goons to whip my ass with a leather strap. God, it hurt like hell! Then I was ordered to bend over a desk so Venchenzo could fuck me. He told me that if I wasn't good, he was going to turn me over to his men for more fucking."

"Holy shit! So he raped you? You can't let this go!"

"No, he didn't. Just as he was ready to shove it in, I flipped around and caught him by the back of the neck and slammed his face into the desk three or four times. Then I tied him up and got my gun and cell back. I made Venchenzo call his goons at a house on 13th Street and order them to take Jack home, unharmed. I called the apartment to verify that Jack was all right and not injured in any way. When I finished talking with him, I made a deal with that asshole Venchenzo. I told him if he closed up the club and left the city and never bothered me or Jack again, we wouldn't press charges. If he chose not to go, we would press charges. He agreed to leave town."

"You're kidding? He's just going to close down and leave the city, just like that?"

"Yes, that's what he agreed to. I also told him if Jack or I ever saw him again, I would kill him without even thinking about it."

"So that's it? You're not going to press charges against this piece of shit?"

"If I did, Jack and I would be looking over our shoulders the rest of our lives. How long would it be before one of his people got to us? No, this is the best way. I've got seven years to press charges, right?"

"Technically, yes, but you'd have a damn hard time doing it more than six months from now. The courts wouldn't look kindly on it."

"I'll take that chance. Please, let's try it my way."

"Okay, on one condition. You come back in there with me while I tell this guy exactly what's up with this shit. He has to have an official police warning. Agree?"

"If you insist, yes."

Dave and Derrick walked into the club where several officers were now standing around and found Venchenzo sitting in a chair, holding a handkerchief to his nose. It appeared that Dave had fractured the gangster's nose, and Venchenzo was none too pleased about it.

As Dave and Derrick walked up to the club owner, Venchenzo stood up, ready to argue if Derrick tried to arrest him.

"Mr. Venchenzo, I'm here to tell you that Mr. Henderson has up to seven years to file any charges that might be appropriate. If you were found guilty of these crimes, the state would incarcerate you for quite some time. Do I understand that you're leaving the city?"

Venchenzo glared at Dave and responded, "Yeah, I've decided the club isn't making enough money here, and I'm going to open somewhere else."

"I see. And exactly *when* will you be leaving our fair city?"

"I'm not sure. But I would expect to leave within a week."

"Very well, then I will assume your club will be closed starting tonight?"

"Yeah. Now if there's nothing else?"

"No, sir, that's all I have. Oh, just one more thing. Stay away from Mr. Henderson and his family. Do I make myself clear?"

"I want nothing to do with the little prick," Venchenzo replied and walked away.

Derrick leaned over to whisper to Dave. "I know for a fact that you are not a *little* prick."

Dave managed to smile before he turned to get out of the club.

"Come on, Dave," Derrick said. "I'll give you a ride home."

JACK charged Dave as he entered their apartment. "Oh my God, I was so scared for both of us! Are you sure you're all right?"

Dave hugged Jack as tight as he could without hurting him. The tension began to ease slightly now that he had Jack in his arms, safe and sound. When Jack pulled his head back, they both had tears in their eyes. Dave kissed him long and hard and then hugged him again.

"Do we have to remain afraid?" Jack asked.

"I hope not. Venchenzo has agreed to leave the city and leave us alone in exchange for our not filing charges against him. Derrick re-emphasized it for him. I also told him that if I ever saw him again, I would kill him."

"This is just all so incredible! I have a hard time believing that I was actually kidnapped and held with the possibility that I could be killed!" Jack said as he moved his hands down and squeezed both of Dave's ass cheeks.

"Ouch! Oh, watch my ass!" Dave yelled out.

"Why? Did you fall or something?" Jack asked.

"No. I didn't really want to tell you, but I figure you'll see it anyway, so I might as well explain. When I got up to Venchenzo's office, he had me stripped, tied down to a bench, and my ass beaten with a strap. They gave me probably sixty blows."

"No! Fuck! Drop your pants and let me look. Have you been seen by paramedics?"

"No. Didn't think it was necessary," Dave replied as he complied with Jack's request.

When Jack saw Dave's ass, he practically screamed and began to cry. "Those rotten fuckers! Your ass looks like raw hamburger! Dave, you're gonna be bruised something terrible!"

"I'll survive, and if it means that piece of crap is out of our lives, then it's worth it."

"Come with me and lie down on the bed. Lemme try and bring you some relief."

"Hmm, not sure that type of relief will do much for the pain," Dave said with a smile.

"Oh my gawd, you can't be *that* bad if your dick is still doing your talking for ya!"

Dave laughed aloud as he walked down the hallway with great difficulty. He took off his pants and shorts and lay down on the bed while Jack got a cold washcloth and brought it back. He put the cloth on Dave's ass, and Dave drew a quick breath of air in reaction to the cool.

Jack pulled a card out of his wallet and made a call.

"Who are you calling?" Dave asked.

"Hello? Yes, I need some medical advice," Jack said on the phone. He then gave the person on the other end his health insurance ID number and asked his question.

"I've have a relative of mine here who was kidnapped and had his rear end beaten with a strap. He thinks he was hit somewhere around sixty or so times. His ass looks all red, has welts, and looks like it's turning purple. What can I do for him?"

Dave turned slightly red at hearing Jack discussing his ass with a total stranger.

"Ah, no, I don't see any breaks in the skin. I'm looking at it now. Generally large welts and sharp red lines where the strap met the skin."

Dave whispered that his ass was now really starting to hurt him.

"He's complaining of increased pain as we speak. Well, the police got him out of there about forty-five minutes ago. Yes... okay, and keep checking on it for infection. I understand... yes, thank you. Good night."

"Well, what's the verdict?"

Jack tried to lighten the mood just a little by answering, "I'm supposed to put your ass in a sling."

When Dave stopped chuckling he replied, "I knew you've wanted to fuck me! You could have just asked!"

"Okay, here's the deal. I'm gonna fill the cloth with ice and gently move it over your ass a little at a time. The ice should take down the swelling. I also have to keep an eye out for any signs of infection over the next twenty-four hours. That's the only real concern. Your ass will look a lot worse than it actually is, but we still have to be careful. You just rest there, and I'll take care of you."

"Thank you, honey," Dave replied, gritting his teeth.

Jack removed the washcloth and went into the kitchen. Dave listened as Jack quickly checked the front of the apartment to make sure all doors and windows were locked. Then Jack turned out the lights in that area and returned to the kitchen. He came back into the bedroom a few minutes later with a soft cloth and a pot filled with ice and water so he could keep the cloth cold. He also brought three aspirin and some iced tea. When Jack put the very cold iced washcloth back on Dave's ass, Dave sucked in air quickly as he dealt with the resulting pain. Jack lit the candles in the bedroom and turned out the light so Dave could rest better.

"Here, take these aspirin," Jack instructed. "They'll help with a little of the pain."

It took over two hours for Dave to begin to feel relief from the onslaught of pain that had been triggered when Jack grabbed and squeezed his ass. The ice began to reduce the surface swelling that had occurred, and Jack removed all of the ice from the washcloth and rinsed it off in the cold water and reapplied it. He kissed Dave on the head and blew out the candles. He then gently crawled into bed and put a pillow between their bodies so that he wouldn't accidently throw an arm or hand over Dave's ass while they slept.

Dave was finally able to fall asleep just past midnight. The one thought that comforted him was that they had the rest of their lives to enjoy good times. He and Jack finally drifted off to sleep.

The next morning, Jack woke up first and climbed out of bed without waking Dave, because he made coffee and brought two cups back to the bedroom where the aroma woke Dave up. "That smells like exactly what I need," Dave said.

"Good morning, honey. How you feel?"

Dave shifted a little and was relieved to feel only a little pain. "Not bad, considering how much it hurt last night. Thank you for taking care of me."

"Well, you know what the preacher man says: for better or worse, in sickness and in health," Jack replied.

"Yeah, I think you just like to look at my ass, tell the truth!" Dave said, and they laughed.

"Well, I do love your beautiful ass, baby, but right now the only thing I want to do to it is make it better."

Dave sipped his coffee and then swung his legs over the edge of the bed so he could sit up. When the weight of his body pressed down on his ass, he winced. As he shifted trying to find a position that would be comfortable, his legs began to shake.

"Honey," Jack suggested, "why don't you just stay on your stomach today and let your skin and muscles recoup? It's not like there's anything you have to get out of bed for, after all."

"Well, it could get messy if I don't get up for *anything*, my dear," Dave replied.

"Oh, well, that's the exception, ya goof. Oh, I'm sure you gotta go now. Want me to help you up?"

"Yeah, just let me lean on you once I get standing."

Jack moved around to Dave's side of the bed and gave him his shoulder to lean on as Dave got up. As the blood rushed down to his lower extremities, Dave winced once again. "Oh, this is gonna be fun. Look, if it doesn't start feeling better by this afternoon, I'd like to go to the hospital."

"Agreed. Come on. Just take it slowly, and we'll get you into the bathroom."

As they walked slowly, Dave began to feel a little better. His muscles needed to be stretched and walking helped that to happen.

When they reached the bathroom, Jack looked at Dave and smiled. "You want me to hold it for you?"

"Ha! Ah, no, I think I can take a piss by myself, thank you."

When Dave was finished, he was able to walk on his own. On the way through the kitchen, Jack asked if he wanted anything to eat. He didn't. He walked down the hallway and turned around and came right back to the kitchen.

"Ya know, honey, I think it would be better if I didn't stay in bed all day. It really is helping to walk around and stretch."

"Okay, just don't overdo it, babe. I know how you like cheese steaks, so I'm gonna go out at lunch and get us a couple of sandwiches. Then, we'll have a light dinner. Sound good?"

"Yeah, I'm always down for munching on a cheesesteak. You know that!"

Dave smiled. He was beginning to feel like his normal self. Now, if that son of a bitch Venchenzo would just leave town in a week like he said he would, all would be much better.

JUST after they had finished eating lunch, the phone rang.

"Hon, it's Derrick," Jack yelled.

Dave picked up the extension and heard Jack thanking him for getting Dave out in one piece. He also told Derrick how much pain Dave had been in from the beating.

"Hey, Derrick, what's up?" Dave asked.

"Just checking on you to make sure you're all right. You didn't tell me that you were beaten last night. I thought the pain I saw you in was from being tied up or something. Are you positive you don't want him prosecuted for what he did to you and Jack?"

"Yeah, we just want him long gone and out of our lives. If all it takes for that to happen is to put up with a sore ass for a couple of days, that's fine. Thanks again for being there last night when I really needed you. I owe ya, guy."

"Yeah, well, it's kinda my job, sport. But if you insist on thanking me personally, I'll think of something when you don't have a sore ass."

Dave could almost hear Derrick smiling. "You are one horny fuck, you know that?" he asked with a hearty laugh.

"Hey, I can't help myself. I've always been a sucker for a handsome guy like you."

"I hear ya. Well, I'll take care of you somehow, babe."

"Okay, I'm gonna hold you to that, stud. Look, if you need anything, call me. Stay safe, both of you. Maybe I'll come by this weekend, and we can watch a movie or something."

"I'd love it, dude. Just let Jack or me know, okay?"

"You got it. I gotta run. Take care."

Derrick hung up, and Dave was grateful for having such a good friendship—a friendship that had begun with a night of hot sex and which usually ended there. Dave thought that he must be slipping. He kept one guy around as a friend, and he made another his lover. What happened to the old "fuck 'em and leave 'em"?

"Everything okay, hon?" Jack asked.

"Yeah, Derrick just wanted to check on me and to suggest that he might come by this weekend to watch a movie here."

"Oh, okay, that sounds like it would be fun. Maybe we can invite one of my cuter friends to join us, and maybe he and Derrick will hit it off, ya know?"

"Oh God, you're playing Suzy Matchmaker. Hey, whatever makes you happy, but if Derrick says he doesn't like blind dates, then just don't do it again, okay?"

"Sure, but you need to learn to trust me, stud!"

"Well, I'll tell you now: Derrick only likes the pretty boys, so do us all a favor, and if you're gonna fix him up, make sure he's a stunner."

"I already figured that out for myself. After all, he got *you* one night, didn't he?"

"Very funny," Dave replied.

A knock on the apartment door brought Jack to his feet and had Dave reaching for his gun. Jack carefully opened the door but left the chain on it until he saw Ron on the other side.

"Hi, Ron, just a second," Jack said as he closed the door to take the chain off. Dave put the gun back in the drawer of the coffee table.

"Hey, guys," Ron said.

"Hey, dude, what's up?" Dave asked.

"I just wanted to check with you to see if you're pissed at me for not waiting until midnight to give that letter to Derrick."

"No, I am definitely *not* pissed off at you," Dave insisted. "You did the right thing, as it turned out."

"Were you in some kind of danger? That's the feeling I got when you ran out of here."

"Yeah, kinda, but I really don't wanna talk about it much because it'll upset me all over again, and I kinda just managed to chill out now."

"Oh, okay, no problem. Like I said, I mainly wanted to find out if we were cool or not," Ron said.

"Oh, we're cool, dude. Don't worry about it."

"Are you okay? Are you hurt in any way?"

"No, I'll be fine. Just a little sore," Dave said.

"Good, glad to hear it. Jack, you're home today! No work?" Ron asked.

"Not today. Dave wasn't feeling real well so I stayed home to play Florence Nightingale."

Dave spoke up. "Listen, Ron, it looks like we're going to have a couple of guys over Saturday night to watch a movie. Wanna join us?"

"Yeah, right now I haven't any plans, so that sounds good. What time?"

"Not real sure yet, as we're just beginning to set it up. But more than likely it will be around eight o'clock."

"Yeah, I'll be here. Any cute guys gonna be here?"

"Well, Jack will be here," Dave responded.

Ron laughed and said, "Well, I can't deny that, but I meant any cute *single* guys; you know, the kind that I might like to date!"

"Well, just put your order in with Suzy Matchmaker here, and he'll see what he can do for ya," Dave said, enjoying the thought of Jack fixing guys up to find what they had found together.

"I'll see what I can do for you, Ron," Jack said with a smile.

"Okay, gotta run. See ya Saturday night, if not before," Ron said, waving and closing the door.

"So what happened?" Jack asked. "Ron took some letter to the cops?"

"I wrote everything down and gave it to him with instructions that he was to take it to the police if he didn't hear from me by midnight."

"Ah, and I take it he went to the cops right away instead of waiting?" Jack asked.

"Yep, he sure did. This is one time I'm glad someone didn't listen to me and did what they thought was best. Otherwise, I would no doubt be sore in other places at the moment... if I were even still alive."

"That means I gotta fix Ron up with one of my cuter friends," Jack said with a chuckle.

Chapter 13

SATURDAY night came, and Jack had once again outdone himself with snacks and drinks. There was an array of different finger foods and desserts, and the bar was open. Dave was feeling almost perfect as the guests began to arrive.

Ron was the first to show up since he lived down the hall, and Jack made him a drink right away. "So Jack, did you fix me up with a cutey or what?" Ron asked.

"I didn't fix up anybody tonight. I've just invited a couple of my friends to join us," Jack replied.

"So who's coming?"

"Derrick, Mark, and Brian. Do you approve?"

"Yes, I approve," Ron responded with a smile.

Dave had finished dressing in very casual clothes and joined Jack and Ron in the living room as the doorbell rang. When Dave returned from answering it, he had Derrick with him.

"Hi, everyone," Derrick said.

Hugs went around with everyone, and Derrick whispered to Dave when it was their turn to embrace. "Are you okay now?"

"Yeah, I'm fine. My ass is black and blue, but it doesn't hurt anymore."

"Good. Just to let you know, the club has been closed, and we don't see Venchenzo's Cadillac around anywhere. We think he's split town."

"I'm glad, 'cause I wasn't kidding. I'd file charges if he didn't live up to the bargain he agreed to." Dave nodded. "Jack tells me he invited a couple of his cuter friends to join us tonight, so maybe you'll get lucky," he added with a big smile.

"Oh yeah? Best news I've heard today," Derrick replied as he shot Jack a smile.

"Okay, what are you two bozos up to over here? You're both looking at me and smiling, which spells trouble," Jack said.

"Nothing, dear," both men responded in unison.

As they sipped their drinks, the doorbell rang again, and Jack got the door this time. When he returned to the apartment, Mark and Brian were with him, and another round of introductions and hugs took place.

"Can I get you guys something to drink?" Dave asked.

"Sure! I'll take a vodka and cranberry, if you have it," Mark replied.

"I'll have the same please," Brian said.

As Dave fixed the two drinks, he couldn't help but check out the two new arrivals who he hadn't met before. They were both in their early twenties, nicely built, with light brown hair and blue eyes. Dave almost spilled the cranberry juice when he got a look at Mark's ass.

"Pay attention to what you're doing," Jack said, coming up behind Dave.

"Huh? Oh, I *am* paying attention, dear."

"Uh huh, you're paying attention to Mark's tight little ass. That would be okay if it weren't for you spilling cranberry juice all over the bar I just cleaned an hour ago," he said with a smile.

"Yes, dear," was Dave's only response. What could he say? He'd been caught. Jack really did have some little cuteys for friends.

Dave checked out Derrick's face and found him totally enthralled with the same view that Dave had been enjoying. Dave smiled again. *Going to be a great night....*

"Here ya go, Mark. Don't spill it now. Brian, here's yours," Dave said as he handed the drinks to the guys who just might turn out to be the party favors.

"Now that everyone is settled in, I'll put on a movie. Everyone okay with the new *Star Trek* movie?" Jack asked.

No one objected, so *Star Trek* it was. Ron and Brian were chatting away, and Dave saw Mark move a little closer to Derrick. Tonight promised to be a very successful night for all involved. Dave knew from talking with Jack that Mark had a thing for cops, and he was sure that was why Mark had worn jeans that were at least two sizes too small.

Dave kept everyone's drink filled throughout the movie, and Jack maintained the snacks at their full level. When the movie ended, Jack offered to put another one on, but everyone voted to just sit and talk. Ron and Brian were getting along just as well as Derrick and Mark. Jack looked at Dave and smiled. Dave knew that Jack was happy that his friends and their new friends seemed to be hitting it off.

At the end of the night, Derrick got up from his chair and pulled Mark to his feet. "Well, thanks for having me over tonight. I enjoyed it, and we have to do this again," Derrick said to Jack and Dave.

"You're not leaving already?" Dave asked with a smile that called Derrick a "dirty dog."

"Yeah, I'm afraid I have to. Been a long week," Derrick said with a smile back at Dave that said, "Yep, gonna get lucky tonight."

"In that case, we'd better get going too," Ron said.

Jack asked, "We?"

"Oh, yeah, Brian is coming over to my place so that I can show him my watercolors," Ron replied.

"Watercolors? Now that's funny!" Dave exclaimed.

"I don't suppose you need a ride home, Mark?" Jack asked.

"Ah, no, Derrick has volunteered to give me a ride," Mark answered.

"Oh, I'm sure he has," Dave said with a laugh.

Jack punched Dave in the arm and said, "Behave!"

Derrick walked over and hugged Dave goodnight, and Dave whispered to him, "Let me know how the night goes." Derrick parted and said, "Of course, bro!"

Everyone else hugged, and then the guys were gone. Dave and Jack were left standing in the middle of the room, which suddenly seemed a lot larger.

"I'll help you clean up, hon," Dave said as he began to gather bowls. It took them only about ten minutes, and everything was back to normal. They shifted furniture back to the way it was before, and they were done.

It was almost midnight when Jack said, "Come on, hon, let me put some more lotion on your poor ass, and then we'll get some sleep."

They went back into the bedroom, stripped down, and climbed onto the bed. Jack grabbed a bottle of lotion that was supposed to help protect and restore damaged skin. As Jack applied the first handful, Dave jerked from the temperature of the lotion. "Damn, that's cold," he said.

"I'm sorry. I'll warm the rest up on my hands before I put it on. You're all black and blue now with a yellow tinge to some of it. But the angry red welts are all gone. I think you're on the mend, finally."

"That feels so good, honey. Work it in," Dave said with a sigh.

After a few moments, Jack finished and washed his hands off. When he came back to the bed, he bent down and kissed Dave on the head and turned the light off. He slid into bed quietly, and they both slept through the night.

MONDAY morning arrived, and Dave was up and showered and fairly recovered from his ordeal at the club. He dressed as he had for the law firm, and after kissing Jack goodbye in the apartment, he walked with him for four blocks until they split up. Jack headed to the bank, and Dave went to the district attorney's office.

They were waiting for Dave when he entered the office for the first time. It was like many D.A.'s offices around the state, overworked with not enough staff. The experience that Dave would pick up interning at the D.A.'s office was just as valuable as the office having another hand.

One of the managers who dealt with interns came up to Dave.

"Good morning and welcome to the Berks County Office of the District Attorney. We're glad you're here," an elegant middle-aged woman said to Dave. "Let me show you to your desk. I'm Helen Dirkhart, and I'll be your official supervisor, though you will be working with others who will direct your work product."

"Thank you. I'd like to thank whoever is responsible for selecting me for the internship. It's a great opportunity for me, and I want to learn as much as possible. Do you know what area I'll be working in?"

"The person who selected you for the internship is the D.A. herself. She went over all the applications and selected who she thought would fit her the best. As for the area of your concentration, it will be a combination of a little trial preparation work and a lot of assistance on cases that are assigned to our investigators."

"Well, I should definitely not be bored."

Helen smiled and pointed to the coffee pot as they passed it en route to the investigations section. They stopped at a desk in the back of the room with a phone on top, a pad of paper, a couple of pens, and nothing else.

"Okay, this is your desk. And the gentleman over there is the person who will be supervising the actual work you do. He's Barry Wilcox, the chief of investigations, and when he's off the phone he'll come over and introduce himself. Now, in this file you'll find your timesheets, which get turned in each Friday. Any questions, just ask me or Barry. Now, may I suggest that you get some coffee and sit tight here until Barry can see you?"

Dave smiled. "Sounds like a good idea."

Twenty minutes later, Barry came over and introduced himself.

"Now, because of the experience you had in the Marine Corps working with the Naval Criminal Investigative Service, the D.A. decided that you would be perfect to help us with our caseload, which I don't mind telling you is quite heavy at the moment."

"Does that mean I'll be spending my day looking up phone numbers and trying to find people on the Internet?"

"Not at all. While that may very well come up, I want you serving subpoenas on witnesses as well as assisting with interviews of witnesses in criminal cases. Depending on how you do at these things, we may expand your job duties."

Dave was pleased to learn that he would actually be of value to the office and not just an errand boy. He had heard enough stories from others in his classes about internships that had led Dave to believe most interns were vastly underutilized.

The hours flew by, and before he was aware of it, the day was over. He left the D.A.'s office a little after five and headed for home since Jack would probably already be there. Dave had hoped to meet up with him and walk home from work with him each day.

When Dave reached the apartment, Jack was preparing to cook dinner. He flew into Dave's arms as soon as he saw him and asked, "How was your first day, dear?"

"It was outstanding. I'm not only going to learn a lot there, but I'm gonna enjoy it," Dave replied.

Jack planted a kiss on him that went on for several seconds. Dave pulled back and looked into the eyes of his partner and smiled. "I missed you today," Dave said.

"How could you miss me when you just said that you liked it there and were enjoying yourself?" Jack asked mischievously.

"Where is it written that I can't miss you *and* enjoy where I'm working?"

"Because missing me should occupy all your thoughts and energy; that's why you can't possibly do both."

"Hmm, I see. Well, maybe I should show you how much I missed you today?"

"Showing me could be a good way to handle this actually. Whatcha got in mind?" Jack asked with a smile as he slipped his hand down between Dave's legs. He pulled his hand back and said, "Damn! You're almost hard down there! You are an ol' horndog, ar'n'cha?"

"Honey, when did I ever claim to be anything else but an ol' horndog? I am what I am, and you make me hard, babe."

"You say the sweetest things."

"Yeah, I know." They both laughed at that, and Jack turned around and turned off the water that he had put on to boil. He took Dave by the hand, and they went into the bedroom. When they got there, Dave tried to take control of the situation as he usually did and was thwarted by Jack assuming the lead.

Jack took Dave's shirt off and licked his nipples slow and easy. He then unbuttoned Dave's pants and lowered them along with his shorts. He had Dave naked within less than a minute of their being in the bedroom.

"Turn around for me," Jack said.

Dave smiled and did a slow turn. When he was once again facing Jack, he had a full erection sticking out. Jack looked him up and down and finally said, "You are one fine piece of ass, you know that?"

"Piece of ass? I hope I'm more than just a fine piece of ass to you," Dave said.

"Oh, you're way more than that to me, babe. The sun has begun to rise and fall on you. But that doesn't change the fact that you are still one fine piece of ass!"

Jack moved Dave over to the bed and sat him down. He took a couple of steps back and slowly removed his clothes, declining an offer of assistance from Dave. When he peeled off his shorts, his hard-on sprung to life, set free from his underwear.

"Hmm, that is one fine cock, lover boy," Dave said as he looked at Jack's cock.

"Yeah? You like what you see?" Jack asked.

"Hell, yeah, I like what I see."

"Can you handle it?"

"Fuck yeah, I can handle it. My throat was made to take your fat cock," Dave said with pride.

"Who said anything about your throat?" asked Jack.

"Huh? Well, my hands are big enough to do anything you want with that, babe," he replied.

"Including guiding my cock into your ass?"

"My ass? Oh. You wanna fuck me?" Dave asked with a look of surprise on his face.

"Yeah, Dave, I wanna fuck you."

"Damn, honey, I haven't been fucked since I let a buddy in the Marines do me when we were in the desert for four months straight. Believe it or not, he was supposed to be straight and married but needed to get some for relief from the tensions of that hellhole."

"Was that the only time you've been fucked?" Jack asked.

"Yes."

"Then get ready for your second time," Jack said with a small smile.

"But honey, my ass is bruised. You don't wanna hurt me more, do you?"

"Your ass is just fine, and I won't hurt you. I promise. You gotta trust me, just like I trusted you."

Dave smiled and said, "How the hell could I say no to you about anything? You're in charge. Tell me what to do, stud."

"First, you're gonna give me head, and then you're gonna turn around and get on your knees and bend over on the bed so that I can fuck you doggy style. That way I won't be putting any pressure on your ass."

Dave licked his lips and looked down at Jack's cock, which was beginning to throb after what Jack had just told Dave he was gonna do to him. Jack walked up to Dave and pushed the head of his dick toward Dave's mouth. Dave opened his mouth and took Jack deep in his throat, and Jack put his hands on Dave's head indicating that he was going to fuck his face before he fucked his ass.

As Jack pumped into Dave's mouth, Dave began to slowly jerk off with one hand and tweak his nipples with his other hand. When Jack saw that, he swatted Dave's upper hand away and replaced it with his own. Jack twisted and squeezed both nipples at the same time as he continued to pump into Dave's mouth.

At one point, Dave had to squeeze the base of his cock because he was beginning to build toward a climax. When Jack noticed, he pulled out of Dave's mouth and bent down to kiss Dave with all the passion he was feeling. It literally took Dave's breath away.

Jack pushed Dave flat on the bed and lay down next to him, continuing the kiss he'd begun when Dave was sitting. As they kissed, Jack began to work Dave's nipples once more, sending shivers down Dave's body and making his cock twitch for attention. Jack broke the kiss and reached down to play with Dave's neglected cock a little. He bent all the way down and took Dave into his mouth, gently sucking and licking Dave's cock. When Jack saw Dave's balls beginning to move, he stopped and sat up. He took a sip from a glass of water on the nightstand.

"Get into the position I told you I wanted," Jack ordered.

Dave smiled and immediately moved. "Remember, you said you would be gentle."

Jack bent over and kissed Dave on each ass cheek and then grabbed the lube. He lubed up his fingers really well and worked the first one into Dave's entrance. He was met with little resistance and was able to move his finger around, stretching Dave as he did. Dave let out a small moan from just this minor stimulation. Jack added a second finger and began to finger-fuck Dave. Dave still had no complaints, and in fact his moaning grew in tone and volume. Jack pulled his fingers out and wiped them off before he put on a condom. He then put a copious amount of lube on his cock and placed the head of his dick at the entrance to Dave's body.

"Like you told me, honey: just relax, and don't fight it."

"I remember. Go ahead, just go slow," Dave cautioned.

Jack began to press forward until the head of his cock popped through. He stopped as Dave sucked in air.

"Damn, you feel like you got a telephone pole there... shit!"

Jack didn't say anything. When Dave stopped complaining, he pushed a little farther in but had to stop again when Dave complained. "Breathe, honey, and relax," Jack soothed. "It's going to feel great. You know that."

"Well, I wish it would hurry up and begin to feel fucking good!" Dave exclaimed.

Jack pushed in a little farther, and after a few more minutes of stop and go, he was in all the way. Now, he just let it rest in Dave's ass as Dave grew accustomed to the intruder.

"Okay, I think I'm good... go ahead slowly," Dave offered.

With that, Jack began to pull out, being careful not to let the head pop out and require a new penetration. He pushed all the way back in and was balls deep without Dave saying anything.

Jack began to maintain a slow pace fuck when finally Dave said, "Okay, go ahead and fuck me like you want. I'm feeling it good now. Yeah, that's it, give it to me faster and harder. Nice!" he said.

Jack was now fully into fucking Dave, and it went on for no more than two minutes because it was just too good. "Shit, I need to come already!" Jack said.

"Go ahead, babe, pound my tight little ass. Give it to me hard just like I do you!" Dave urged.

After another six thrusts, Jack came hard and arched his back from the force of the climax. When he was spent, he pulled out slowly so that Dave's ass could relax. They collapsed onto the bed together in a heap of sweaty flesh and the complicated emotions raised as they once again joined in the act of sex. Jack was panting in an attempt to regain control of his breathing. Dave was enjoying the feelings generated by Jack repeatedly hitting Dave's prostate.

"I love you," Jack said.

"Honey, I love you too. That was some great sex we just had. Fuck!" Dave replied.

"I'm glad you liked it. I'm not going to want to do that often, but I needed to do it at least once."

"Why wouldn't you want to do it all the time if it was that good?" Dave asked.

"Because, you're the top... not me."

"Oh hell, honey, that has nothing to do with it. If you want ass, you just have to ask for it. Fuck this top or bottom shit!" Dave said.

"No, you miss my point, hon. I kinda look at you as being the one in charge, you know, the dominant one. I know that if I really wanted something or insisted on something, that you would give it to me, but I *like* the idea that you're the top."

"So that means you don't wanna fuck me?" Dave asked, trying to understand.

"Right. I love the head you give and the other ways I get off when we're making love. I look at anal as your privilege, if you will," Jack said, trying to explain. "And most of all, I like the idea that I *can* fuck you if I want."

"Okay, I can't say I understand, but it's like this: if you want ass, you can have ass. You just ask for it. Otherwise, I'm quite happy to be the one doing the butt fucking around here," Dave said, with a loud laugh ending the comment.

Chapter 14

THE rest of the week went as quickly as it had begun. Jack and Dave were invited to Derrick's house on Saturday night to play cards. As he and Derrick talked, Dave learned that Mark would be there as he had been for most of the week.

"If Mark is going to be there, I take it that your date went well last weekend?" Dave asked.

"Yeah, you could say that," Derrick replied while laughing.

"I want details. Did you do the nasty with him?"

"Hell, what do you think? He took off his clothes faster than I did for you!"

Dave laughed at the memory. "Well, then what?"

"Well, he had a killer body, nice dick, on the smaller side, but a very hot ass."

"And…."

"Damn, but you're nosy! I fucked him. What do you think? I certainly didn't bring him home to play Monopoly with."

"So he was good in bed then, huh?"

"Oh yes, and just as good the next five times."

"Damn! That has to be a record for you… with the same guy. Damn, I'm impressed. But I kinda knew that was going to happen when I got a look at his fine little ass."

"Yeah, well, I took a picture of him nude. If he says it's okay, I'll share it with you."

"And what if he becomes your boyfriend? You'll have showed me a nude picture of your boyfriend."

"Big deal. We'll all probably end up skinny-dipping someplace in the future."

"You're the man! So what time? Say eight o'clock?"

"Yeah. Sounds good. And I'll order a couple of extra large pizzas, so don't eat big before you get here, okay?"

"Sounds good, stud. See you tomorrow night," said Dave.

Dave was still smiling at the thought of Derrick having all that fun with Mark when Jack walked into the room.

"Okay, what are you up to now?" Jack asked.

"Nothing, honey. Just had a chat with Derrick. He really hit it off with your friend Mark, and we're invited to his house tomorrow night for cards. Mark will be there, by the way."

"I know," replied Jack.

"How do you know? I just got off the phone with Derrick."

"What? You don't think that Mark and I talk? I call him from work, and we chat or go out to lunch now that I don't go out to the campus on Wednesdays anymore. I've heard all about how Derrick is some big stud and knows just how to ring Mark's bell."

Dave smiled. "Yeah, that's what I understand. Come over here, sexy."

"What?" Jack asked with a smile as he walked over and sat down with Dave.

"Nothing, I just had a question to ask you."

"Damn, I knew you were up to something. You're not going to ask me to have a foursome with Derrick and Mark, I hope," Jack asked with a raised eyebrow.

191

"What? Why the hell would you think I was going to ask for that?"

"I saw how you were ogling Mark's ass, and I know how much you like to fuck guys! Thought maybe your buddy was offering up my friend as a party favor."

"I am shocked—just shocked, I tell you! That kind of a thought would never cross my mind."

"Uh huh, bullshit. But if that's not the question, what's on your horny little mind, my dear?"

"Well, you know that I love you very much. You're cute, you're good in bed, you can cook, and you complete me. You make me wonder how in the hell I made it this far without you by my side. When I think of the future, you're in it. When I think of growing old, you're in it. And when I think of the end of life, I pray that you're still in it when I leave, because I don't wanna be alive after you're gone," Dave said as tears welled up in his eyes.

"Dave, what's the matter? Why are you getting so emotional? Is there something you're not telling me?"

"I'm telling you how much you mean to me and that you've become part of my very life force. I wanna ask you a question."

"Dave, you're scaring me. You know I feel the same way about you. I think we're both very lucky to have found each other. This entire Venchenzo mess made me very fearful that I was gonna lose you to him somehow."

"There wasn't a snowball's chance in hell that you would lose me over that scumbag. Hell, I was even willing at one point to let him have what he wanted just to leave us alone."

Jack kissed Dave on the lips and said, "I know, honey. I'm so glad you didn't have to do that. Well, what is it that you wanna ask me then?"

Dave reached down behind the cushion of the sofa and brought out a black velvet box. When he opened it, Jack found himself looking at a solitaire diamond ring that was just over one full carat in weight. Jack gasped in surprise.

"Oh my God, what have you done, Dave?"

"Jack, will you marry me and spend the rest of your life with me?"

"What! Oh my God, yes, I'll marry you!" Jack said and threw himself on top of Dave and kissed him deeply. Then he sat up and took the ring box and looked at it even closer.

"Dave, this is beautiful! Is it real?"

Dave laughed out loud. "Of course it's real! Do you really think I would ask you to marry me and then give you a fake rock? Here, lemme put it on you."

Dave took the ring out and put it on Jack's left ring finger and found that it fit perfectly.

"How did you manage to buy the right size?" Jack asked.

"I took one of your older rings with me to the store, and they took the measurement from that. So you like it?"

"What's not to like, honey? It's brilliant in color and looks right at home on my finger."

Jack once again threw himself into Dave's arms, kissing him on the lips and down both sides of his neck. Dave put his arms around the man he loved and squeezed.

"God, I love you. Promise me you'll never leave me?"

"Hell, baby, I'm gonna marry your ass. You just try and get rid of me!"

"I figured we could go up to Massachusetts to get married since the Commonwealth of Pennsylvania is still run by the ignorant. Is that cool?" Dave asked.

"Hell, yeah. We got a wedding and honeymoon to plan! Who's gonna be your best man? Like I really have to ask."

"Probably Derrick. I really like him, and we have a lot in common."

"Yeah, you both like to fuck cute guys," Jack said with a laugh.

"Well, that, too, but there's a lot more than just that. In fact, with my new job, I may even get to work with him on something."

"Well, I'm gonna ask Mark since he's just about the best friend I've ever had. So they both can participate in the wedding."

"Anything you want, honey. Where would you like to spend your honeymoon?" Dave asked.

"Oh, that's a great question. What are my choices?"

"Anywhere in the world. I figured we can drop a total of five grand on everything and still have plenty of money in the bank."

"Lemme think about it. When are we actually gonna get married?"

"How about next month? We'll make it around mid-October? Is that okay?"

"That'll work great. I have just shy of two weeks' vacation that I have to use before the end of the year, so that works out fine. What about you and the internship, though?"

"Under the terms of the internship, I get to take up to one full week off anytime during the course of employment. So, I'll just take a week off around that time, and we'll go."

Jack smiled as he thought about it all, and the more he smiled, the closer he moved his hand up Dave's leg to where Dave's prominent bulge was showing.

"Come on! Let me show you how happy I am by giving you the best blow job you've ever had!"

"I don't know... I've had some pretty damn good blow jobs. Are you sure you're up to that task?" Dave asked with a wicked smile.

Jack didn't say another thing. He let his mouth and tongue do his talking without having to say a word.

THE next night Jack and Dave arrived at Derrick's right on time to play cards. After they greeted each other with hugs and kisses, everyone got settled down to play cards. Derrick poured drinks, and they sat down at the table.

Jack was first to deal and as he slid out the cards, Mark noticed something sparkly.

"Oh my God! What is that on your finger?" he asked while grabbing Jack's hand.

"Oh that? Just a little something my trick gave me," Jack replied with a smile.

"Trick, my ass! That is something your *fiancé* gave you," Dave roared out.

"Fiancé? You guys are getting married?" Derrick asked.

"Yes, and I'd like you to be best man," Dave replied.

"Hell yeah, I wouldn't miss it for the world. When and where?"

"Massachusetts, around the middle of next month if the dates work out right for everyone," Dave answered.

"Mark, I'd like to ask you to be my best man as well. Will ya?" Jack asked.

"I would be so pissed if you asked anyone else that I probably wouldn't speak to you again," Mark answered.

Everyone got up and there were hugs all around once more. Forgetting the cards, they moved into the living room and sat down where they continued to talk about the plans that had been made so far.

THE second weekend of October found Jack and Dave driving up to Boston, accompanied by their best men, Derrick and Mark. Everyone was in a great mood, and they couldn't wait for events to unfold. Dave and Jack had to apply for the license on Monday and wait three days before picking it up from City Hall. Then they could get legally married.

They pulled into the Sheraton Boston, checked into their rooms, and took a quick nap. They planned on having dinner and then hitting the bars a couple hours later. During dinner, Derrick made his own announcement.

"Here's to the two you, may you have many long happy years before you," Derrick said as he raised his glass in toast to Dave and Jack.

"Thank you, my friend. Jack and I really appreciate your coming to Boston to witness our marriage vows and to celebrate our happiness with us," Dave said in return.

After they all took a sip and set their glasses down, Derrick said, "I have an announcement to make. I am pleased to tell you both that Mark and I have decided to become a couple. As of now, we are officially lovers," he announced with a smile.

Mark sat there and beamed at his new lover. Jack was patently surprised. It appeared that this time, Mark hadn't let Jack in on the good stuff. "I can't believe it! You? Mark? Have settled down? The entire city of Reading is now going to go into shock," Jack said as everyone laughed.

"Well, like you guys found out, when it's right, it's right. Mark is pretty special, and I have to admit, I wasn't really happy being single. We think we can build a great future together, and we'd appreciate it if you guys were there to help us get through the sticky parts and to enjoy the happy parts with us."

"Derrick, you know that I think you're one hell of a guy, and I couldn't be happier that you've found each other," Dave said. "Whatever we can do, man, just let us know."

"I have to say that I wish Derrick would find another line of work," Mark said. "I'm afraid I'm going to fit right in with that worried spouse image that many cops have in their lives. One thing you can count on is that Derrick always goes to work with his bulletproof vest on."

"Mark, I think Derrick is a well-trained police officer, and we'll all just have to count on that training to keep him safe. Try to think only positive thoughts and enjoy each other."

"So where are you guys going on your honeymoon? Have you decided yet?" Mark asked.

"Well, we'll only have a few days left after we get married to do anything. It takes, as you know, three days just to get the license. So the wedding is on Thursday, and we both have to be back at work on Monday. What we've decided to do is put off the honeymoon until next year when we have the time to take an all-gay cruise to the Caribbean," Jack answered.

"Maybe one day we'll be attending your wedding," Dave remarked.

"Ya never know!" said Mark.

THE next day, Dave and Jack stood in line at Boston's City Hall. They were one of twenty couples lined up at that moment and one of two gay couples. They filled out the paperwork, paid the fee, and left to return to the hotel. Derrick and Mark were awake and about to order breakfast when Dave and Jack joined them. Together, they had a room service breakfast of eggs Benedict and hash brown potatoes that put everyone in a great mood for the rest of the day.

When Thursday morning came around, Jack picked up the license from City Hall and returned to the hotel. Everyone was dressed and waiting for Jack to dress as well so that they could head to a small Old Catholic church near Harvard University. There, a very young and attractive priest waited for their party to arrive.

"Well, is everyone ready?" Derrick asked.

"Yep. Here are the rings for the ceremony," Dave said as he handed him a ring box containing both gold bands.

"Great. I'll try not to lose them between here and the church," Derrick said with a smile.

"Where are we going to have our wedding night dinner anyway?" Mark asked.

"We've got reservations at six forty-five at a real nice Italian restaurant that has outstanding food. I ate there about five years ago, and I swear they had the best caesar salad that I've eaten anywhere," Dave said.

"Sounds great! Let's get going before we're late for the church," Derrick said.

AS THEY entered the church, Dave got butterflies in his stomach and felt lightheaded. Derrick saw him change color and whispered to him.

"Are you okay? You don't look good."

"I'm fine. I just got hit with the full realization of what's about to happen. Because I'm gay, I never thought I would ever be able to get married. Now, here we are, and I have a legal license to wed the man I love."

Jack walked up just as Dave finished speaking. "It is rather surreal in many ways, honey. You're not thinking of changing your mind are you?" Jack asked.

"Change my mind? Hell no! I'm just overcome with the feeling of achieving one of life's goals for men and women. I've found my guy, and this step crystallizes in my mind just how important this day is to us. Many people have fought hard and long to deny us this right, to deny us this joy, and yet, here we are walking down the aisle."

"Many people have fought long and hard to *give* us this right, as well. It's just one more reason that for gay couples getting married is so very important. We owe it to ourselves and to them," Jack said.

"Excuse me, are we about ready?" the priest asked.

They walked up the aisle and stood before the priest, who took the marriage license and looked it over. He smiled and said, "All right, everything looks good. Shall we begin?"

"Please," Jack responded.

The ceremony was over in five minutes, and Jack and Dave were legally married in some states and ignored in others. But none of that mattered to the couple for the marriage had occurred within their hearts and souls as well as in the church with a license. This needed no acknowledgement by man or woman because they were now one. What's more, they felt like they were now one.

Dave knew they would pursue their rights with various government bodies, but the ontological change had occurred, and that's what really mattered. Their love would go on to support them and see them through the good times as well as the bad. They faced the world now as a joined couple and no longer as just individuals. Together, there was nothing Jack and Dave could not accomplish... especially for each other.

JOHN SIMPSON, a Vietnam-era Veteran, has been a uniformed Police Officer of the Year, a federal agent, a federal magistrate, and an armed bodyguard to royalty and a senior government executive. He earned awards from the Vice President of the United States and the Secretary of the Treasury. John has written articles for various gay and straight magazines. John lives with his partner of 35 years and three wonderful Scott Terriers, all spoiled and a breed of canine family member that is unique in dogdom. John is also involved with the Old Catholic Church and its liberal pastoral positions on the gay community.

Visit John's web site at http://www.johnsimpsonbooks.com/.

Also by JOHN SIMPSON

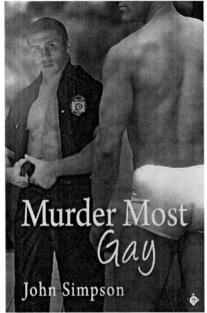

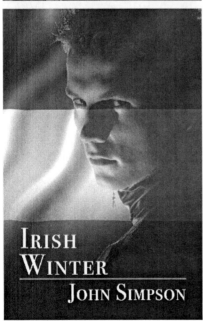

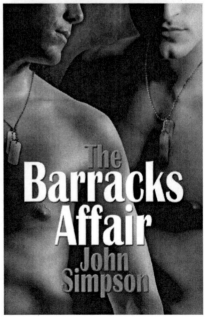

http:/www.dreamspinnerpress.com

Contemporary Romances from

DREAMSPINNER PRESS

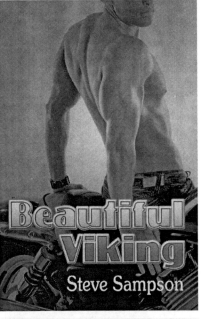

http://www.dreamspinnerpress.com